THE SHORE ROAD MYSTERY

When the Hardy boys eagerly agree to assist their friend Jack Dodd and his father in locating a family treasure, the two young detectives are unaware of the baffling complications that will arise. The only clue to the long-lost treasure is a cryptic message written by a Pilgrim ancestor.

But when Mr. Dodd and Jack are accused of stealing cars and then mysteriously disappear, Frank and Joe are confronted with a triple mystery. Have their friends run away to avoid the law? Or are they secretly hunting for the treasure? Or have they been kidnapped?

Despite mounting evidence and the bitter suspicions of the townspeople, the Hardys are convinced that the Dodds are the victims of a sinister plot. Clues that Frank and Joe uncover, with the aid of their jolly, plump friend, Chet Morton, lead to the secret hideout of a ruthless gang of criminals.

Deadly road traps and aerial ambush, a spider man and a suspect who carries a menacing cane harass the young detectives as they seek the triple solution to this perplexing and exciting mystery.

Joe flew into the air

THE HARDY BOYS

BY FRANKLIN W. DIXON

THE SHORE ROAD MYSTERY

Grosset & Dunlap
An Imprint of Penguin Random House

GROSSET & DUNLAP
Penguin Young Readers Group
An Imprint of Penguin Random House LLC

Penguin supports copyright. Copyright fuels creativity, encourages diverse voices, promotes
free speech, and creates a vibrant culture. Thank you for buying an authorized edition of this
book and for complying with copyright laws by not reproducing, scanning, or distributing any
part of it in any form without permission. You are supporting writers and allowing Penguin to
continue to publish books for every reader.

Cover illustration by Matthew Taylor.
Cover design by Mallory Grigg.

ISBN 9780515159080   10 9 8 7 6 5 4 3 2 1

CONTENTS

CHAPTER I

Pursuit!

". . . *stolen at Dune Beach. Car is Swiftline cream sedan, believed heading south on Shore Road. Alert all cars! Repeat . . .*"

The bulletin had just come over the police band on Frank Hardy's motorcycle radio. He and his brother Joe, side by side on their dark-gray machines, were roaring northward along Shore Road to join school friends for a swim.

"Dune Beach!" Frank shouted, and the boys skidded to a halt on a sand shoulder. The car thief might pass them at any moment!

"Let's stop him!" Joe proposed.

The boys waited, scanning a deserted fishing pier on their right. Frank was eighteen, tall and dark-haired. Joe, a year younger, was blond. Both were excellent amateur detectives.

"Joe, do you realize this makes five car thefts in one week along Shore Road?"

The Hardys steered their motorcycles to the land side of Shore Road and faced them south, ready to move out quickly.

Several cars whizzed by, heading north. Then two police cars screamed past in the other direction.

After five more minutes had gone by, Frank frowned. "It looks as if *we're* not going to nab any thieves today."

Joe said, "Let's hope the police are on the right track!"

But subsequent bulletins indicated another successful getaway by the car thieves. The Hardys cycled to Dune Beach to learn what they could. Here the boys found several state troopers taking down information from the elderly man whose car had been stolen.

"It was gone when I came up from the beach," he said.

Presently the boys headed south for their swim. "I don't understand this," Joe remarked. "The stolen car couldn't just vanish into thin air!"

"The police seemed just as puzzled," Frank observed. "Unfortunately, there were no witnesses. Did you notice that the tires of two nearby cars had been punctured? The thief must have done that to avoid pursuit."

The brothers eased their motorcycles toward a wooden rack behind Oceanside's bathing pavilion. Joe swung off his vehicle and unstrapped his towel roll. "Maybe a good swim will sharpen our wits."

"Right," said Frank as they headed for the bathhouse.

Being the sons of Bayport's famous detective, Fenton Hardy, the boys were not easily deterred by initial disappointments in pursuing criminals. Although still high school students, they had helped their father on many cases and had used their sleuthing prowess in solving several mysteries. Joe, though impetuous, was quick-witted and dependable. Frank, more serious-minded, was inclined to think out a situation before taking action. They worked well together.

After the Hardys had changed into swimming trunks and Bayport High sweat shirts, they trotted across the hot white sand to the roped-off bathing area.

"Frank! Joe!" called their waiting friends.

Greetings were exchanged as Phil Cohen and Tony Prito, pals of the Hardys, bounded over from behind the lifeguard's green chair. Phil was a quiet, intelligent boy with sandy hair. Tony, olive-complexioned and lively, owned a motorboat and had shared many adventures with the Hardys out on Barmet Bay.

"We're sorry," Frank apologized, "but we were delayed by a car thief." He recounted the story.

"Another one!" Tony shook his head. "Is your dad on the case?"

Joe slipped off his sweat shirt. "No, not yet. He's going out of town today. All the police in the area are, though. Maybe there'll be a break in the mystery soon."

Phil tilted his head. "If you fellows get on the job, there will be." He grinned. "For better or worse."

"Thanks," said Joe, then turned and raced for the water. Frank followed.

"Whoa there!" From behind a pair of sunglasses appeared the tan, smiling face of blond Lifeguard Biff Hooper.

The Hardys greeted Biff and looked around the beach. There were not many bathers in evidence.

"Where is everybody today?" Frank asked.

"I think the car thefts are keeping folks away," Biff answered. "It's been like this for a week."

"Have any of the rest of our crowd been here today?" Joe put in.

"I haven't seen Iola all day," Biff teased.

The others laughed, and Joe joined in. Bashful with girls, he was used to being teased about his attachment to Chet Morton's sister.

"Say, where's Chet?" Frank asked.

"Chet? I haven't seen him here this week," Biff replied. "But I did hear he's been spending some time at the Bayport Museum."

"It must be connected with food." Tony grinned. Their stout friend loved to eat.

Frank and Joe went swimming. An hour later

they saw Biff beckoning to them from shore. "Message for you fellows!" he shouted. They swam quickly to the beach.

Biff exclaimed, "A phone message was just brought to me! Jerry finally got his new car! He's at Beach Grove. Why don't you Hardys run over later and take a look at it?"

"Great!"

Jerry Gilroy, a fellow student, had long spoken of buying a handsome car for which he had been saving earnings from summer and after-school jobs.

Before leaving, Frank and Joe decided to stroll along the beach toward a black stone jetty in the distance. Suddenly they came upon a dead bat in the sand.

"Funny," said Joe. "Wonder how that got here."

The boys walked on to the end of the jetty and scanned the horizon. Beyond the bathing area, a black fishing boat cruised by slowly. Moments later, the Hardys recognized a smaller green-and-white boat which belonged to their friend Jack Dodd.

They waved to him. Jack seemed about to wave back when they saw him lurch forward sharply and drop below in his boat. Then he stood up and signaled frantically.

"Something's wrong!" Joe gasped. "Look! The bow is beginning to list!"

The Hardys dived off the jetty and swam swiftly out to meet the craft as Jack headed it toward the rock promontory. In moments they had climbed into the boat.

"Frank! Joe! Quick! In there!"

Jack pointed to the small forward compartment as he maneuvered the boat closer to the jetty. Below, the Hardys found themselves standing in an inch of churning water!

"Near the left bulkhead!" Jack called down, cutting the motor.

Frank had already spotted a small, bubbling fount and covered it with his foot. Joe ripped a towel off a hook and together they stanched the leak until some wood sealer was found in the paint locker. By the time Joe and Jack were mooring the boat to the jetty, Frank had tightly plugged the leak.

"I guess I owe you fellows my boat." Jack smiled gratefully as the three bailed most of the water out of the compartment.

Jack Dodd was a likable, dark-haired youth. He and his father, a widower and respected Bayport citizen, worked a farm on Shore Road.

"The exercise did us good—and in." Joe laughed and jumped onto the jetty. "How did it happen, Jack? Did you strike a rock?"

Jack shook his head worriedly. "Some other object struck my boat underneath."

Frank's face showed astonishment.

"Something's wrong!" Joe gasped

"It sure seemed that way. I was moving along great until I heard a scraping noise and then the gush of water. I've never hit any rocks around here before."

"But who would deliberately—" Joe was puzzled.

"You've got me." Jack shrugged. "I've run into some cranks along the coast, but never any who seemed likely to do this sort of thing." A gleam came into Jack's eye. "Say, how would you fellows like to help Dad and me solve a mystery?"

"A mystery!"

"Yes," Jack continued, brightening. "My uncle, an astronomy professor at Cheston College, is coming up from Greenville tomorrow to assist us, but we need a couple of good local detectives." He grinned at the Hardys. "This mystery concerns a geographical puzzle that's been puzzling our family for three centuries!"

The Hardys whistled. "You bet we'll help!"

Jack promised to give them the details the following day. He cast off, waving good-by.

After Frank and Joe had changed into their sport clothes, they returned to the motorcycles and headed north on Shore Road, eager to see Jerry's new car.

As they neared Beach Grove Point, they saw a boy running toward them. "It's Jerry!" Frank exclaimed.

The Hardys screeched to a halt as their wiry,

red-cheeked friend flagged them down. His hair was tousled and his eyes wide with worry.

"The car—my new car!" he gasped. "It's just been stolen—sky-blue Cavalier hardtop! Did it pass you heading south?"

The brothers shook their heads. "Then it must have gone north," Jerry declared.

"We'll chase it," Joe offered.

The Hardys gunned their motors and swept northward. Crouching low, they whipped up an incline beneath a rock overhang.

"There it is!" Frank shouted.

Several hundred yards ahead a light-blue hardtop sped around a long curve in the highway. When the car came into view again, the gap between it and the boys had widened. The Hardys accelerated and streaked ahead through an unbroken stretch of farm country.

"We're gaining on him!" Joe yelled.

He had no sooner said this when Frank saw something that made him exclaim in dismay.

A huge, bright-red produce truck pulled out of a dirt road directly ahead, entirely blocking off the highway! It stood still.

"Joe, look out!" Frank shouted, desperately braking down from top speed.

But it was too late! Tires smoking, the motorcycles screeched into a skid off the road!

CHAPTER II

Police Tip-off

SWERVING to avoid a wooden fence, the Hardys windmilled their motorcycles violently. Both boys flew off as the machines came to a stop in a cloud of dust. Dazed, Frank pulled himself up and limped over to Joe.

"You okay?" Frank asked with concern. His brother had a bruised forehead and had skinned his left arm.

Joe seemed stunned but managed a weak smile. "I just hope our cycles came out of it as lucky as we have."

"The radio's banged up," Frank said.

Up ahead, the door of the produce truck slammed. A short, plump man with yellowish-white hair approached the Hardys. From his floppy straw hat, denims, and mud-stained shoes the boys concluded that he was a farmer.

"You fellers all right?" he asked. "Mighty sorry

'bout that spill. Didn't see you comin'. My truck horn don't work noways. Hope you wasn't in no hurry."

"We were after somebody, but it's too late to catch him now," said Frank. "May we use your phone?"

"Ain't got one," the man replied.

As he drove off, the Hardys righted their motorcycles. To their relief, both machines were operable.

"We'd better get back to Beach Grove," said Frank, and the boys chugged off.

They found that Jerry had already phoned the police. There were no noticeable footprints or other clues where he had left his car.

"I sure hate to lose that bus," Jerry said. "Although the car was a year old, it was a good one, and an expensive model, too."

"Was your car locked?" Joe asked their friend.

"Yes, but the thief managed to get it open."

After the police arrived, Frank and Joe said they must leave. Jerry thanked the boys for their efforts. "I'll let you know what happens," he promised.

In a short time the brothers reached the pleasant, tree-shaded Hardy home, which stood at the corner of Elm and High streets.

After dusting off their motorcycles, the boys entered the back door and tiptoed through the fragrant kitchen.

"I'm ready to put away a good meal," Frank remarked.

Smudged, unkempt, and with a few bleeding cuts, they hoped to wash before alarming their mother or peppery Aunt Gertrude. Their father's unmarried sister was a frequent visitor.

They had no sooner started up the stairs when Miss Hardy came from the living room and called to them.

"Supper is almost ready—" In the moment of silence that followed, there was a disapproving gasp. "Frank and Joe! Look at yourselves! Dust and mud and dirt and—" the tall, angular woman began.

"That supper sure smells good, Aunty!" Joe said, smiling.

"Joe Hardy, don't you change the subject!" she continued. "A fine spectacle you are! And tracking dirt all over your mother's vacuumed carpet—"

Suddenly Aunt Gertrude saw Joe's skinned arm and bruised forehead. "Joe, you're cut! And Frank—why are you limping? Oh, my goodness, what happened?"

Her nephews could not repress smiles. They soon dispelled her concern without mentioning the details of their accident on Shore Road. The brothers loved their aunt and knew that beneath her huffish way she held great affection for them.

"Well, maybe you didn't track the carpet too

badly," she said. "But, Joe, you'd better put some antiseptic on that ugly scratch. Frank Hardy, be careful going up those steps!"

Later, the boys joined the family at dinner. Their mother was a sweet-faced, quiet woman. Mr. Hardy was tall and distinguished looking.

After hearing the details of the day's happenings, the detective announced that he was leaving for New York on business. He left the table before dessert was served and hurried upstairs. Presently he reappeared, set a suitcase in the hall, and prepared to say good-by in the dining room.

"A big case, Dad?" Frank asked him.

"Not big enough, son." The detective grinned. "After that last shirt was packed, I had to stand on the case to get it shut." The pun brought pretended groans from his sons.

Their father went on, "I'll be in New York City, perhaps for several weeks. Authorities there have asked me to work on an arms-smuggling case. The smugglers are apparently supplying American criminals with foreign-made lethal weapons."

"Got any leads, Dad?" Joe asked.

"Not yet. The government is greatly concerned over their distribution."

Mr. Hardy kissed his wife and sister good-by. Then Frank and Joe accompanied their father outside to wait for his taxi to the airport.

"Too bad about Jerry's car," the detective said.

"Chief Collig asked my help on the theft case. Unfortunately, I had already accepted the New York assignment."

"Do you mind if we have a try at the Shore Road mystery, Dad?" Frank asked hopefully.

"It sounds like quite a challenge—even for my sons!" He smiled. "But I think the police could use any help available. Take care of yourselves and keep in touch. By the way, put my car in the garage before you go to bed. It's in the driveway."

"Sure thing, Dad," said Frank.

Back at the table, the brothers discussed the day's events with the women. "I wonder why Jerry's stolen car was headed north," said Frank. "The other Shore Road thieves always turned south."

Just then they heard a familiar voice from the kitchen door.

"Hi, Chet! Long time no see!" called Frank.

Stout, good-natured Chet Morton appeared, eating a piece of celery he had picked up from the kitchen table. Chet's visits to the Hardy household at mealtimes were not a rarity.

He greeted Mrs. Hardy and Aunt Gertrude, then said, "Hi, fellows!" Chet dropped into Mr. Hardy's vacant chair. "Sorry I couldn't meet you fellows at the beach today, but I've been kind of busy with my work."

"Your work?" Joe repeated. Work was not one of Chet's strong assets.

He reached for an olive as Mrs. Hardy said, "How about some dinner? I'll get you a plate."

"Not tonight, thanks, Mrs. Hardy."

Aunt Gertrude raised her eyebrows. Seldom did the stout boy turn down an offer of food!

Frank and Joe hid smiles behind their napkins. Finally Frank urged, "Come on, Chet, something's in the air. It's not like you to—"

Joe was not paying attention. He interrupted to say, "Listen! I just heard a noise from the driveway. It sounded like a door of Dad's car being shut!"

The three boys rushed out to the back porch. "Look!" cried Joe.

A hulking figure was getting into Mr. Hardy's sedan. Another man was already in the car.

"Stop!" Frank ordered.

Tearing down the steps, the boys ran across the lawn. The men jumped out and dashed down the driveway to the street. In an instant they were picked up by a waiting car, which roared away. The boys gave chase but to no avail. Identification was impossible because the driver had put out the lights and the license number could not be seen.

"Pretty daring thieves!" Chet commented. The boys hurried back to Mr. Hardy's automobile. Finding no damage, Frank drove it into the garage and locked the door.

"Those guys sure had a nerve trying to steal a

detective's car," Chet remarked as they re-entered the house. "Any special reason, do you suppose?"

"They probably didn't know Dad's away," said Frank, "and thought this would handicap him if he should be working on the car thefts."

"This may have been our first look at some of the Shore Road gang," Frank concluded.

After reporting the attempted theft to the police, the boys went to the living room, where Chet proceeded to explain his latest project.

"I'm studying dietary survival." He took a book from a pocket and tapped the cover. Chet brought a carrot from another pocket and bit loudly into it before tossing the book to Joe. Its title was *Vegetable Survival in the Wilderness*.

"Sounds interesting, Chet," he said. "But what brought this on? You've always been the biggest eater in Bayport High."

"Common sense," Chet intoned. "You see, we live in a dangerous world, never knowing where our next meal may come from. So, I figure to learn a little botany in case I'm ever marooned on a jungle island or too far from a hot-dog stand. In other words, herbivorous survival."

"Herb—" Frank stared.

"Plant eating, for you laymen," Chet said, nibbling a second carrot. "I've decided to live on vegetables and fruits between visits to the museum and library to study."

"And how long is this going to go on, Chester

Morton?" demanded Aunt Gertrude as she came in. "No more chocolate fudge cake—ever?"

Chet shifted in his chair and swallowed. "I haven't worked out the—er—details yet, Miss Hardy. It depends upon my—er—further research."

Frank grinned as his aunt shook her head in puzzlement and left the room. "Well, we sure wish you luck, Chet," he said. "Sounds pretty austere to me."

"I'll make it," Chet declared. "Tell me about your swim."

The Hardys told their friend of all the adventures on Shore Road that afternoon, of their plans to help Jack Dodd, and of the theft of Jerry's new car.

Chet's eyes bugged out. "Wow! I sure feel sorry for Jerry. I hope the police catch those thieves."

Later, as the boys were listening to a television newscast, the speaker said the police had not yet apprehended the thieves.

"Sure is a tough mystery," Chet remarked.

Frank suggested they all look at a map of the Shore Road area. "Maybe we can figure where the cars disappear to."

Just then the telephone rang. Joe took the call, then rushed back to the others.

"That was Jack!" he exclaimed. "He sounded upset and wants us out at the farm right away!"

Suspecting a sudden development in Jack's

secret mystery, the three boys piled into Chet's green jalopy and headed out Shore Road. As they pulled into the dirt lane to the Dodd farmhouse, they saw the rotating red lights of police cars in front of the house.

"Something has happened!" Joe exclaimed.

Officers and excited reporters were assembled near the front of the big porch, while three patrolmen stood by an empty car near the back of the house. The hum of car engines filled the night air.

After parking, the Hardys and Chet found Mr. Dodd and Jack standing next to a state trooper at the side of the building. The thin, well-dressed farmer, who had a slight mustache, looked pale and worn. Jack's hands were clenched.

"The Hardys! And Chet!" Mr. Dodd exclaimed, forcing a smile as the boys rushed up to them.

"What has happened?" Frank asked immediately.

Jack hung his head and pointed to the unoccupied automobile. "We've been accused of stealing that car!"

"Stealing!"

"Yes," Mr. Dodd continued grimly. "Jack had just discovered this car on our property tonight when all these officers began to arrive—apparently having received a 'tip-off' over the phone that *we* were the Shore Road thieves."

A husky, uniformed man, Chief Ezra Collig,

approached the group and greeted the Hardys. Mr. Dodd tried to recall the whereabouts of himself and his son on the day the car was reported stolen.

Jack added, "We couldn't have stolen the car on that day, sir. Both Dad and I were—"

At that moment his attention was diverted by an approaching officer. In his hand he carried a fishing pole.

"Is this your rod, son?" he asked.

Jack stared in surprise. "Yes, but—"

"Then what was it doing in the trunk of the stolen car?" the officer demanded.

CHAPTER III

A Pilgrim Mystery

"My fishing pole—in the stolen car!" Jack repeated in disbelief. "It's been missing from my boat since yesterday."

Chief Collig examined the rod, then frowned. "Personally, I'm inclined to believe you, Jack. But I'm afraid you and your father will have to come to headquarters. We particularly want to check the fingerprints on the car."

"Fingerprints?" Joe queried.

Mr. Dodd nodded resignedly. "I'm afraid you'll find my fingerprints inside. I got into the car, hoping to find the owner's name in the glove compartment."

Frank spoke in low tones to Chief Collig as flashbulbs illuminated the area. The chief assured him the Dodds could be released on bail until a hearing, but said the figure would probably be a very high one. The Hardys promised to visit Mr.

Dodd and Jack the next morning about their release.

"We'll contact Dad right away," Frank told the Dodds.

Chet added, "Jack, keep your chin up!" He drove the Hardys home, where they wired their father.

The following morning the brothers drove to Bayport Police Headquarters to see Mr. Dodd and Jack. As they had feared, the bail figure was too high for the Dodds to pay it all at this time.

"Frank!" Joe exclaimed as the boys left the building. "Maybe Dad will help them out with the rest!"

Over the telephone, Fenton Hardy supported the boys' faith in the Dodds' innocence and promised to arrange by phone for the balance of the bail payment. Shortly after noontime the two prisoners were released.

"We can't thank you boys and your father enough," Mr. Dodd said as Frank was driving them back to their farm in Mr. Hardy's car. "Having your father's name behind us at the hearing tomorrow will mean a great deal."

"We're glad to do what we can." Joe grinned.

"Have you any idea who might have wanted to frame you?" Frank asked as they headed north.

"Not really," Jack replied. "But Dad and I have come up with one possibility."

"His name is Ray Slagel," Mr. Dodd explained.

"He came to the farm looking for work about a month ago. But he didn't prove dependable, and after I had found him away from his chores several times, I had to dismiss him."

"Did you have any trouble with him after that?" Joe asked.

"No," Mr. Dodd answered, "but he threatened to get even with me. I can't tell you much about his background, but we can describe him."

"Dad," Jack interrupted excitedly, "I think I still have that picture I took of Slagel!"

"That might give us something to go on," Frank remarked. "Actually, we've got two Dodd mysteries."

"I almost forgot!" Jack gasped, remembering his uncle's expected visit that night.

Mr. Dodd laughed. "Frank and Joe, are you still interested?"

"Interested!" the Hardys cried in unison. "We sure are!"

Frank turned the sedan off Shore Road onto the lane leading to the Dodd house. Mr. Dodd and Jack cordially invited the Hardys inside, where they all sat down in the attractive, pine-paneled living room. Over a large flagstone fireplace hung a framed black-and-white map of the Atlantic coast. There were several early Colonial prints above the bookcases and sofa.

"We're ready for the story," said Frank.

"As you may know," Mr. Dodd began, "the Dodd family, while small today, goes back several hundred years in this country." He pointed to some faded, brown-leather volumes along a mahogany shelf. "There are records in these of centuries of Dodds—records that go back before the Revolutionary War. Unfortunately, they tell us little about the man at the root of the Pilgrim mystery."

Frank and Joe leaned forward.

"We do know," the farmer continued, "that in the year 1647, one Elias Dodd embarked from Plymouth Colony in a small skiff with his wife and three children. A good seaman, with considerable knowledge of astronomy, he went in search of a horseshoe-shaped inlet he had heard of from an Indian. Dodd hoped to establish a settlement to which other families might come later."

"A horseshoe-shaped inlet!" Joe exclaimed.

Mr. Dodd smiled. "The inlet that is today Barmet Bay."

"Did he reach it?" Frank asked.

Mr. Dodd stood up and paced the room "That is the mystery we hope to solve. You see, Elias Dodd was never heard from again. But many years later, a bottle was found washed up on a shore farther south of here. In it was a note believed to have been written by Elias before he and his family perished in a sudden, violent storm.

"Deterioration of the paper had obliterated some of the words. In the message, Elias hastily described their last geographical position."

"And you have the message here?" Frank asked.

"Only in our heads." Jack smiled.

Mr. Dodd explained. "My brother Martin, who teaches astronomy at Cheston College in Greenville, has the original. You'll be able to see it when you meet him this evening."

"And you're hoping," Joe said, "to discover whether your ancestor perished in the Bayport area?"

"That's right, as well as to determine the existence of the Pilgrim treasure."

"Treasure!" Frank and Joe echoed.

Jack's father went on, "When Elias left the colony for his journey, he brought with him a chest of jewels, many of which were very valuable. He hoped to use the less expensive ones to barter with the Indians he might encounter."

"Because of the treasure, I assume the mystery must remain in confidence," Frank said.

Mr. Dodd nodded. "Dishonest people mustn't hear about it," Jack said. "They might find the chest before we do. And there is the possibility it contains his journals which would also be valuable."

Frank and Joe stood up as Mr. Dodd glanced at his watch. Though eager to hear details of the Pilgrim clue, they realized that Jack and his father needed a chance to obtain legal advice for their hearing the next morning on the stolen car.

Frank shook hands with the Dodds at the front door. "We look forward to meeting Martin Dodd —and seeing the old paper—tonight!"

Jack smiled, fingering a rabbit's-foot key chain, but his face seemed to cloud with the anxieties of last night's events. "Thanks again, fellows," he said. "Without you, we wouldn't even be free to work on the mystery."

"As it is," Mr. Dodd added, "we must solve it within the next few days!"

His mention of a deadline puzzled the Hardys. He promised to explain later that night.

Jack gave the boys a photograph of Ray Slagel. The picture revealed a burly, bald man leaning on a pitchfork before the Dodd barn. He wore a work glove with a V-shaped cuff on his left hand.

The Hardys then drove out to Beach Grove where they locked the car and began combing the sand for clues to the thief of Jerry's stolen car. Later, they heard Chet's jalopy arrive, and he joined the brothers in the search.

"I guessed you fellows would be here," he said. He took out a large magnifier. "Thought you could use a botanical consultant. Say, do you think the evidence against the Dodds is serious?"

"It could be," Frank admitted, kicking into a small mound of sand. "They have no witnesses for their whereabouts the day that car was stolen, but

Mr. Dodd's good reputation can't be discounted."

Chet leaned down with his magnifier at the top of a sand slope to inspect a plant. Suddenly he lost his balance, and rolled down the incline.

"Chet, are you all right?"

Their rotund friend regained his feet. Scrubbing sand out of his hair, he held up a glove. "This might be a clue!"

Frank and Joe went down to look at it.

"It's a work glove!" Chet said, pointing to the V-shaped cuff.

At that moment the boys saw a car slow down on the road above them. They raced up the slope, but when they reached the highway, the car was already disappearing around the bend.

The boys rushed to check their cars. Neither had been tampered with.

"Wonder what he was looking for," Joe remarked.

"Maybe the same thing that Chet found," Frank said. "Joe, have you that picture of Slagel?"

Joe produced the photograph. Frank compared the left-handed glove Chet held and the one in the picture.

The two looked identical!

"This may be the lead we're looking for!" Frank rejoiced as they walked to their cars.

"Do you think this could help prove the Dodds' innocence?" Chet asked.

"It might if they can identify it as Slagel's when we see them tonight."

Elated by the clue, the Hardys thanked Chet and headed home. After a light supper, they told of their proposed visit to the Dodds. Aunt Gertrude was skeptical about the bail which Mr. Hardy had put up so promptly. "You're all too trustful," she said. "Look up this Slagel in your father's files."

Frank and Joe did so, and were disappointed when the files revealed no information on Slagel.

"Reckless, plain reckless, Frank and Joe Hardy," Aunt Gertrude said. "Why, the Dodds may really be car thieves!"

"But Dad doesn't think so, Aunty," Joe reminded Miss Hardy.

"Never you mind. You just can't rely on men who don't have a woman around the house to keep them straight." Despite her words, the boys' aunt was secretly proud of their magnanimous efforts to help the Dodds.

When the telephone rang, Joe answered the call. "It's Chief Collig," he whispered to Frank. Then Joe's jaw dropped and he slowly hung up the phone. He could hardly speak.

"The chief says the Dodds may have jumped bail. They've disappeared in their station wagon!"

CHAPTER IV

Suspicious Visitor

PERPLEXED over the news of the Dodds, Frank and Joe immediately cycled out to the farm. It was a scene of confusion, with a crowd of spectators watching the excitement from the highway.

"There's Chief Collig," Frank indicated as the boys parked next to a bright-blue television van. They went over to speak to him. As they walked with him toward the house, Joe asked, "But why would the Dodds run away ?"

Collig took a deep breath and shook his head. "I only know they appear to have left hastily— and, I'm afraid, permanently. One of our patrols noticed the garage was empty and investigated. The door of the house was unlocked. All food and clothing were gone."

The officer turned to the boys. "I'm sorry that you and your dad will suffer financially should the Dodds not appear at the hearing tomorrow."

Frank and Joe, in their concern over the Dodds, had completely forgotten about the posted bail.

The police chief accompanied them through the farmhouse rooms. Joe, who was familiar with Jack's room, noticed that a pup tent and sleeping bag were missing.

"I don't understand it," Frank said ruefully as they started down the stairs. "Jack seemed worried but not enough to—"

"I'm afraid this isn't all," Collig interrupted. He held out a large rabbit's-foot charm. "Have you boys ever seen this?"

"Yes, that's the one Jack had on his key ring," Joe said.

"Another car was stolen at Bay Bluff during the last hour." Collig hesitated. "This charm was found there."

When the three returned to the noisy scene outside, the boys inquired for Jack's uncle. He had not arrived.

Frank and Joe decided to ride out to Bay Bluff. As they reached their motorcycles, Frank said in a low voice, "Joe, I have a hunch that Jack and his father didn't leave of their own accord."

Joe whistled. "You mean they might have been kidnapped? But why—"

The discussion was interrupted by the arrival of a short, stout man named Oscar Smuff, wearing a green tweed suit and Tyrolean hat. He appeared to be taking copious notes in a memo book.

Smuff, an aspiring detective, had long wanted to become a member of the Bayport Police Department. The Hardys often encountered him on cases, but he was not distinguished for powers of deduction or insight. The boys greeted him and started their vehicles.

"Too bad about all that bail money," Smuff said. "But you're just kids—didn't know you were backing car thieves. Got in over your heads this time. Should have asked my advice.

Joe was about to retort, but Frank signaled to him and they wished the egotistical detective good night.

Heading through a cool sea wind down the dark highway, the Hardys soon reached Bay Bluff. Near a lone police car, a young woman was wiping her eyes as an officer spoke with her. The boys parked and introduced themselves.

From the woman's story, Frank and Joe gathered she had parked at the bend, heading south, and climbed a foot path to watch the sunset. "I did leave the key in the ignition," she admitted, "and my car wasn't visible from the path, but I had a complete view of Shore Road traffic in both directions. Then I saw my car moving out on the highway—but it was too late."

"We're sure sorry to hear that," said Frank.

After the policeman and the woman had driven away, the Hardys looked for clues to the theft. The stolen car had been driven south toward Bayport.

Frank followed his flashlight beam across the road toward the ocean. Joe did the same. From far below came the sound of the pounding surf.

"If only Jack and Mr. Dodd had known about the glove we found!" Joe sighed. "Now, it may not be wise to publicize that we have it until we have some idea where Slagel is."

Frank agreed. "But it might be good for us to have a talk with Dad tomorrow. If—"

Frank's voice was drowned in a loud screeching sound as a limousine burst around the bend from the south. It swung too wide in the turn and headed straight for the boys!

Blinded by the glaring headlights, Joe slipped but sprawled safely out of the way as the big car rocked back onto the road and raced off. Frank had vanished from sight!

"Frank!" Joe cried out, rushing to the edge of the bluff. He heard a sound, and looking down, was relieved to see his brother's hands grasping the vines of a small bush. In a moment he had pulled him up.

"Whew! Thanks!" Frank gasped. "I was standing on an awful lot of air down there! Did you get the license number of that car?"

"No," Joe replied. "But it looked to me like a tan Carlton, two or three years old."

After a double-check failed to turn up any clues, the brothers headed home. Mrs. Hardy and Aunt Gertrude were upset to hear of the Dodds' disappearance. Their mother also mentioned having heard prowlers outside the house earlier in the evening.

"Again! Were they near the garage?" Joe exclaimed.

"Yes," Aunt Gertrude replied. "I looked around out there myself but didn't see anybody. Your father's car was not touched."

"Joe, the glove!" Frank started, suddenly remembering that they had left it in their crime lab over the garage.

Both boys tore out of the house and ran up to the lab. The pine-paneled room also served as a combination workshop and clubhouse. One maple bookcase, a small safe, several plaster footprint molds, and various scientific kits were arranged neatly along two walls of the lab. Hanging on another wall were assorted disguises—wigs, beards, masks, and hats.

Joe flicked on the light and opened a cabinet. *The glove was gone!*

Frank groaned. "Our only clue! But let's make a duplicate of Slagel's picture, anyway."

They did this, then returned to the house.

"Well," Joe said, trying to be cheerful, "the Dodds may still show up at the hearing tomorrow."

A light came into Frank's face. "Joe! We may have lost a clue, but I think we've gained something in its place."

"What?"

"The fact that the glove was stolen from us proves it must be important—and probably to Slagel!"

The late news reports gave no word on the missing Dodds, but another car had been reported stolen and presumed to have been driven toward Bayport. When the announcer read its description, Joe jumped up.

"A tan Carlton! Frank, it's the car that almost ran us down at the bluff!"

"But the driver was heading *north*. Still—" Frank snapped his fingers. "I've got it! Tire marks prove the thieves always head south. But what's to stop them from turning around a minute later and heading north?"

"A simple U-turn!" Joe agreed.

The following morning, just before the scheduled hearing of the Dodd case, Frank called Chief Collig and learned that the Dodds had failed to appear. Nothing had been heard from Martin Dodd, either.

"Do you suppose he was kidnapped too?" Joe asked Frank.

His brother shrugged. "If so, it may involve the Pilgrim mystery. Let's go out to Cheston College and make some inquiries."

Before they left, a phone call came from their father. After briefing him on the latest developments, Joe asked, "Dad, how's your case coming?"

"I'm not at liberty to say much, but I wouldn't be surprised if I suddenly took up the study of gases as a hobby. I wish I were free, though, to give you boys a hand."

Late that morning Frank and Joe traveled by train to Greenville, then walked to the peaceful, shaded campus of Cheston College. At the office they learned that Martin Dodd, a bachelor, had left as expected the day before for Bayport. The boys obtained two photographs of the astronomy professor. Both showed him to be tall and middle-aged, with a gray mustache and horn-rimmed glasses.

"He may be in Bayport right now," Frank remarked hopefully.

But when the Hardys called on Chief Collig later that afternoon they were told nothing had been heard of the mysteriously missing uncle. Without mentioning the Dodds' Pilgrim mystery, the Hardys provided the chief with one of the professor's photographs.

"We'll look for him," the officer promised.

Upon reaching home the brothers found that Mrs. Hardy and Aunt Gertrude were out. A few minutes later the boys received a visitor. Frank ushered the heavy-set, well-dressed man into the living room. He introduced himself as a Manhattan businessman.

"I must profoundly apologize for not giving my

name to you boys," he said. "I have come on a matter of a highly confidential nature."

"My father can't help you now. He is away," Frank told him. "Perhaps when he returns—"

"Oh, but you misapprehend me," the stranger protested, removing his spectacles. He smiled ingratiatingly. "It is the services of the distinguished sons of Fenton Hardy which I am interested in acquiring—for a private case in New York City."

The stilted language and pompous manner of the man impressed neither of the boys. Suspicious of his wish for anonymity, they informed him that they were engaged on other matters. His flattering persistence availed nothing.

"You refuse then? Most unfortunate, most unfortunate," the man whispered. He bowed curtly at the door and left.

"There's something fishy about him," Joe commented. "Too bad we couldn't get his name."

"I did notice some things," Frank said. "The cigarette he was smoking was a foreign make, and that gaudy tie clasp had the initials C. M. on it."

"Maybe he wants to get us out of Bayport!" Joe suggested.

Other thoughts crossed the boys' minds. Was the stranger connected in any way with the Shore Road thieves? Or did he know anything about the disappearance of the Dodds?

Early that evening Joe phoned Chet, and without disclosing details of the Pilgrim mystery, told him of the missing Martin Dodd. Chet agreed to come to a strategy meeting at the Hardy home the next day.

Joe had just hung up when he thought of something. "Frank! Jack's boat! We forgot all about it! Do you think the Dodds could have gone off in that?"

"Not unless their station wagon is parked down by the boathouse. But we might find some clues there to where they could be!"

Ten minutes later Frank and Joe reached an aluminum boathouse at the Bayport waterfront. They parked their motorcycles. Faintly pink clouds lingered in the sky below a rising half-moon. Over the distant hum of cicadas, the boys' footsteps drummed on the wooden boards of the dock.

Inside the dark, oblong structure six boats were moored. Eerie shadows seemed to ripple up the corrugated walls from the lapping water. At the end of the row, Frank saw a green-and-white boat bobbing gently.

"It's still here!" he said.

Joe, snapping a finger to his lips, grabbed his brother's arm. He had heard a sound outside, but now only the wash of water on the hulls came to their ears. The brothers worked their way along until they stood over Jack's boat. Holding the damp railings, the Hardys peered into its dark hold.

"Let's have a closer look," Frank said.

At that moment the sound of a board creaking came from inside the cabin of the boat.

"Joe! Somebody's in there!"

Before they could investigate, the boys felt strong arms around their necks. Wet cloths were slapped over their faces!

CHAPTER V

Strategy

FRANK awoke to see blurred reflections from the water on the dark boathouse ceiling. His clothes felt damp, and he was conscious of a heavy feeling in his head.

As Joe stirred alongside him, Frank scrambled to his feet, then helped his brother to get up.

"Jack's boat—it's gone!" Joe said groggily. "Did you get a look at the men who attacked us?"

"No, but whoever grabbed me and clamped that cloth over my face was strong. Wonder what knocked us out?"

"Some kind of liquid gas is my guess," Joe answered.

After informing Chief Collig of the attack upon them and the stolen Dodd boat, many unanswered questions filled the Hardys' thoughts as they drove home. Who were the men who had gassed them and taken the Dodd boat? Could they have been

Shore Road thieves, who also had planted a stolen car at the Dodd farm? Did they know anything about the clue to the Pilgrim treasure? Above all, what had become of Jack and his father?

Frank looked worried. "We feel sure the Dodds aren't car thieves, and what happened tonight at the boathouse makes me think more than ever that they didn't run away."

"You mean they were not only kidnapped, but maybe harmed?"

"That's right," said Frank. "Tomorrow let's forget the car thieves and start a hunt for Slagel."

The next morning Frank and Joe worked on their battered short-wave radio, then cycled into town. When they reached the Bayport business district, the boys paused for a moment at the corner of Main and Larch. Frank gave Joe one half of a penciled list of hotels and rooming houses and the copy of the Slagel photograph they had made.

"Righto," said Joe. "See you in an hour at this corner."

The boys separated, Joe taking the north end of Bayport and Frank the south. An hour later neither Hardy had yet come across a Slagel registered in any of the hotels. None of the desk clerks had recognized the photographs.

During the second hour, Joe had no success. Only five names were left on his list.

"You have any luck?" he asked Frank hopefully when they met to compare progress.

Frank wiped his brow. "Not a thing. I covered all the waterfront places and saw the registers myself. How about you?"

"No."

Frank read down his list. "Well, this last run ought to do it. Fingers crossed!"

But the boys' final circuit turned up no leads. Disappointed, the brothers headed through the center of town for home.

"Slagel may still be in the area, but staying in another town," Frank remarked.

"At any rate," Joe declared, "I guess we'll have some more footwork cut out for us."

At the Dock Street traffic light Joe noticed a heavy-set, well-dressed man getting into a taxicab.

"Frank! That's our nameless visitor from New York!"

The brown-and-white cab pulled out and headed toward the western side of town. The boys decided to follow on their motorcycles.

Moments later, the taxi wound under an overpass and came to a stop at the Bayport railroad station. Parking nearby, the Hardys followed as the man purchased a ticket in the waiting room, then boarded a waiting New York train.

Joe heaved a sigh. "Well, we can cancel one lead—at least for the time being. Maybe he was telling the truth about living in New York City."

Frank and Joe found Chet at their house. Presently the three boys went to the brothers' crime lab.

Chet proudly dropped a large cylinder of paper on the table. "I thought we could use this to find the car thieves."

"What is it?" Joe asked.

Chet rolled out a highly detailed map of Bayport and its environs. "It's on loan from my father's real-estate office."

The Hardys marveled at the map's detail, which included geographical features as well as houses and roads in the entire Shore Road area.

"This is a great help, Chet!" said Frank.

After switching on an overhead fluorescent light and locking the door and windows for security, he rejoined the boys over the map spread out on the table. The three pored over the paper for the next half hour. Except for the sounds of Chet chewing gum, the room was silent.

Two considerations were paramount: Where were the Dodds, and where were the stolen cars being taken?

At last Frank sat back. "I have a hunch that working on the thefts is the only way we'll ever find Jack and his father. With the Dodds missing, suspicion of future thefts would naturally fall on them."

"Do you think their lives are in danger?" Chet asked.

"I'm afraid so," Frank replied. "They may be prisoners within a few miles of where we are this minute. The gang may be making a quick haul of flashy cars, and storing them at a hideout until they can be safely moved. But as long as the thefts continue, I think the Dodds will be kept prisoners."

Since Chet was to be a part of their sleuthing team, Frank and Joe now told him about the Pilgrim mystery.

Joe paused at the window. "I feel that the treasure also would fit right into the disappearance of Jack and his father and even the uncle," he commented. "If only we had a copy of Elias Dodd's last message! Do you think Slagel or the car thieves found out about the treasure and kidnapped Jack and his father to keep them from looking for it?"

"It's possible," Frank answered.

Moments later, Mrs. Hardy interrupted briefly to give the boys four letters which had come for them in a late delivery. As Frank and Joe read them, Chet noted their grim expressions.

"Who sent the letters?" he asked.

"They're complaints," Frank replied. "Some townspeople aren't happy about our backing the Dodds."

Joe slapped the letter he was reading. "This one is from a theft victim. He even says he'll hold us responsible if the Dodds aren't apprehended!"

"People are really getting up in arms about

these thefts," Frank said. "We must work harder to track down the thieves."

First, the boys reviewed recent copies of the *Bayport Times* for theft evidence, which proved to be scanty. Then they studied minutely the mapped roads leading to and from Shore Road.

"There are a few things that seem certain," Frank concluded. "One, the thieves appear to be after late-model cars, and to steal most of them at night. Two, the gang can't be a small one—their success alone would suggest that. And three, the stolen cars are most likely driven *north* up Shore Road."

"If," Chet cut in, "your U-turn theory is right."

"Correct. The police have suspected a southerly direction so far, and therefore have been concentrating on watching Bayport. But as the papers indicate, patrols are now keeping an eye on other towns that lie off Shore Road to the north."

Chet shrugged. "Then what could we possibly learn that the police haven't?"

Frank drew the others' attention to the black line which represented Shore Road on the map.

"The thief heads north. He *could* go straight into Northport, but he'd take a chance staying on one road all that distance. This leaves the turnoffs which meet Shore Road from the west."

"I follow," Joe murmured.

"Now," Frank continued, "police have been watching all towns at the end of the turnoffs, but there's one place they haven't been stationed—at the intersections themselves!"

He went on to propose a two-part plan. "With daily night watches, at the Shore Road intersections with Springer Road, Route 7, and Pembroke Road, we should find out which one the thieves are using! Daylight hours we can spend sleuthing around the terrain off Shore Road, since the gang may have a secret hideout in the woods."

Chet whistled. "Boy, night watches, day watches, and three mysteries rolled into one! There goes my important museum work!" He groaned loudly as Frank and Joe grinned.

"But, Chet, this will give you a chance to do some real field work for your botanical and dietary investigations," Joe explained, slapping his heavy friend on the back. "Think of all the herbs and plants in those woods!"

Chet was weighing the idea when they heard familiar footsteps ascending the garage stairs and a sharp rap on the door.

"I've brought you boys some refreshments," came the voice of Gertrude Hardy.

"Refreshments!" Chet echoed happily, opening the door. The laden tray Aunt Gertrude carried looked inviting.

Noticing the closed windows she winced. "A beautiful day like this and you three sitting in a hot, stuffy room! Frank, Joe, here are some apple pie and chocolate milk."

A heavy object sailed through the window

"Oh boy!" Chet exclaimed.

"And for you, Chet Morton, a large glass of cooling parsnip juice. I fixed it especially for your vegetarian diet."

"My vegetarian—" Chet's voice trailed off despondently at the sight of the liquid.

Muffling laughs, Frank and Joe thanked their aunt. "Your pie is—"

Suddenly there was a deafening crash. A heavy object sailed through the rear window, sending splinters of glass against Joe's neck. Chet flew from his chair and Aunt Gertrude screamed.

In the center of the floor lay a black hand grenade!

"Run!" she cried.

But Frank knew that in a few seconds all of them might be killed! He snatched up the grenade and ran to the window with the deadly missile. Would he be able to hurl it outside in time?

CHAPTER VI

Mysterious Collision

THE others watched in frozen horror, fully expecting the grenade to go off in Frank's hand. The next second he tossed it from the broken window. Everyone stood as if in a trance, waiting for the explosion.

But it never came.

The boys and Aunt Gertrude drew shaky sighs of relief. "Must be a dud," said Frank. "I'll check."

He ran downstairs and around to the rear of the garage. He immediately spotted the grenade lying in the grass. With his foot he gingerly turned it over. In the bottom gaped a round, unplugged hole. "It's a dummy, all right," Frank said to himself.

Next, he looked about for any signs of the grenade thrower. There was no one in sight and no clues to the person's identity. Quickly Frank picked up the grenade and returned to the lab.

Aunt Gertrude, recovered from her fright, was highly indignant. "I don't care if that—that bomb is a fake! What a wicked thing to do! The villain responsible should be tarred and feathered!" She paused for breath. "Frank, you were very brave, but you shouldn't take such chances!"

Her nephew smiled. "I'll try not to, Aunty."

With a warning for the boys to be extra cautious, Miss Hardy left. Chet and Joe had by now swept up the broken glass and the young sleuths turned their attention to the grenade. Joe lifted it and studied the hole closely.

"Look, there's a note where the firing pin should be!" He unrolled the paper and the boys read the typed words:

*Keep off Shore Road or next time this will
be a real one.*

The message was unsigned, and when they dusted the grenade it showed no fingerprints except the Hardys'. The weapon was clearly of foreign manufacture.

"Think Slagel threw it?" Joe suggested, recalling the missing glove.

"Or one of his pals," Frank replied. "At any rate, our conference wasn't overheard. What say we start today on our two-part plan?"

After the window had been boarded up, the Hardys and Chet started for the door. Joe grinned. "Chet! You forgot to drink your parsnip juice."

"Oh—er—yeah, I almost forgot," he muttered, plodding over to the table. Grimacing, he downed the liquid, choking on the last few gulps.

"Good?" Frank asked, chuckling.

Chet wiped his lips and beamed at the brothers before leading the way vigorously down the stairs, the map under one arm.

"Nutritional!" he called back.

Chet rode at the rear of Joe's motorcycle as the three boys headed for a wooded area near Springer Road. This was the most northern of the three roads they suspected as the thieves' possible escape route.

The trio spread out and began combing the area for clues. There was little traffic this far north. The air was close, and the pitch pines afforded little shade.

In white sneakers and saggy dungarees, Chet trudged along between the Hardys. He occasionally consulted a botanical handbook.

They reached farmland and doubled back along the edge of the woods. Finding no tire marks or buildings, the boys returned to the motorcycles and rode a few hundred yards south. They began combing another patch of trees.

Five minutes later the trio heard a noise behind a thicket-covered hill. Frank motioned for silence and the boys hid behind a large rock.

The crunch of turf became louder. When the person had almost reached the rock, Frank revealed his presence.

"Well, Frank Hardy! And Joe, and Chet! What brings you city fellers all the way out here?"

"Scratch! What a surprise!"

Before them stood the disheveled figure of Scratch Cantrell, a well-known local drifter and long-time acquaintance of the Hardys. Scratch lived alone in the woods. Under a straw hat and ragged gray overcoat, he wore brown trousers, patched in several places. Two pieces of clothesline provided him with suspenders, and rusty sewing scissors, with which he shaved, were tucked into a belt loop. The boys explained their interest in the Shore Road mystery.

"Have you noticed any cars in the woods around here, Scratch?" Frank asked.

Removing his hat, the drifter scratched his wispy hair. His voice was gravelly. "No, haven't seen none. But I've *heard* 'em."

"Heard them?"

"Yep, about two days back. I was just waterin' down my campfire when I heard a motor in the woods, then a noise like a crash. Didn't find nothin'. Sounded like a siren on the highway later."

"The siren may have been the police pursuing one of the stolen cars!" Joe observed.

But they were puzzled by Scratch's story, particularly the mention of a "crash." Unfortunately, the grizzled man could not remember where the incident had occurred.

Scratch did recall something else, however. "I saw a man drive out of these woods the other day, and another time walking along Shore Road."

Frank asked what the man looked like.

"Big guy, bald, kinda mean-lookin'. Wasn't happy when I seen him pullin' out of the woods."

Quickly Joe took out the picture of Slagel. "Is this the man?"

Scratch nodded. "He had a walkin' stick. Don't know why he was carryin' the cane—he didn't seem to limp."

Encouraged by news that Slagel had been in the area recently, the boys thanked Scratch and returned to the motorcycles. Soon they were cruising homeward.

Chet felt weary from their trek and lack of food. "But I'm going to keep on with my vegetable juices," he declared valiantly.

Joe grinned. "Here's luck!" He pretended to drink a toast.

Presently Frank remarked, "I have a hunch we'll be meeting Slagel soon." At that moment he saw something on the beach that made him stare in astonishment. "Look! Two men are tied up down there!"

Flashing across the road, the Hardys stopped their motorcycles abruptly, then rushed down to the two men. They lay behind a dune, and had been visible from the road for only a moment. From their clothing, the boys believed they were fishermen. Both were distraught. One of them pointed to the north as Joe untied him and ripped the gag off his mouth. "We were jumped and our car stolen. Can you fellows catch that thief?"

"How long ago did it happen?" Frank asked as he freed the other man.

"Two—three minutes—a brown Condor with white wall tires."

Frank groaned, realizing they had passed the car moments before! "We could never catch him now, unless— Joe! Let's try the old Pine Road shortcut!"

While the fishermen hurried toward a farmhouse to alert the police, the Hardys and Chet raced to the motorcycles.

"Will I slow you down?" Chet puffed anxiously.

"No." Joe motioned for him to get on. "But hold tight—don't lean back!"

They sped along the highway for a quarter mile, then chugged up a dirt rise to the old overland route. This was stony and overgrown, but a shorter way to the north.

Through the clouds of dust, Joe and Chet could barely make out the crouched form of Frank ahead. Chet held on tautly.

"Heads!" Frank cried back, as Joe and Chet barely ducked under a broken oak limb.

Minutes later, they came out to the highway. He'd still have a lead on us, but we may be able to catch him now," Frank murmured.

They proceeded north, passing several cars. Whizzing beside pastures, they approached a cloud of dust at the Pembroke Road intersection.

"Come on! Let's try the turnoff!"

The boys took the curve, squinting for a glimpse of the stolen brown car. Suddenly they heard a crashing sound!

"That came from the woods!" Joe exclaimed, staring to his right.

They proceeded slowly among the trees until they came to some tire tracks. Seeing no car or evidence of a collision, the boys followed the trail. At a turn in the tracks, Frank noticed something on the ground. "A clue!" Here and there were flecks of brown paint. He scooped them up and wrapped them in a handkerchief. The trio continued following the tracks, but they only led the boys back to the highway.

"Beats me," Frank said. "Whoever drove in seems to have driven right out again. But why?"

On the way back, they dropped off the paint flecks at the police station for analysis.

At the Hardy garage Chet pulled a gnarled mass of broken leaves and stems from his dusty pocket. "My plant specimens!" he groaned. "Ah, what scientists must suffer—and all for nothing! Fellows, could we postpone our first night watch until tomorrow? I'm tired—and hungry."

The Hardys agreed, feeling sorry for their chum. After Chet left, the brothers had supper and opened a special-delivery packet which had arrived that afternoon from their father. To their surprise, it contained data on Slagel.

"Dad is sure a wonder!" Joe declared.

Information on the man's recent moves was scant, but the report said that Slagel had been dishonorably discharged from the Army and had served a prison term in Leavenworth. A list of several aliases was given, as well as an indication he had been born left-handed, but now used either hand.

Later, while the boys were studying a small map, the doorbell rang. Mrs. Hardy answered it. When she came back into the living room, their mother seemed perplexed.

"That's strange. A man was at the door. He wore a blue winter face muffler and didn't identify himself. When I told him that your father wasn't at home, he seemed hesitant. Finally, before leaving, he asked me to give this to you boys." She handed Frank a small, white envelope.

On the front of it was the drawing of a bottle!

CHAPTER VII

Flight Sniper

IMPATIENTLY, Frank tore open the envelope and removed a folded message. It was a photostat of an aged, incomplete message. He read it aloud:

" '. . . *when the ſtorm broke . . . alone . . . to give our poſition in the hope that . . .*' "

Frank glanced at Joe. "The Dodds' Pilgrim clue! Each small *s* looks like an *f*, the way an *s* was written centuries ago!"

He continued. " '. . . *vegetation no protection . . . ſhelter but craſh of countleſſ . . . breaking black illowſ . . . high vein of gold . . .*' "

In the margin was a crude drawing of a leaf. Frank passed the paper to his brother. "That's all. Looks as if part of it has been cut off at the end."

The brothers spent the rest of the evening trying vainly to interpret the message and speculating on the identity of the visitor.

"As I make it out," Frank remarked, "the storm in this message is the hurricane in which Elias Dodd perished with his family."

"And the question is, where?"

"Apparently they found some cover, for it mentions vegetation. If only we knew what kind. The leaf drawing must be a clue."

Joe tapped his head with a pencil. "But if Elias Dodd's bottle washed up on the shore, wouldn't the family have been out at sea?"

His brother had second thoughts. "There's something about the words 'vegetation' and 'shelter' that suggests a location on land. Besides, wouldn't Elias Dodd have needed some kind of shelter in which to write the note?"

"That figures," Joe replied. "What do you make of the last part?"

Frank reread the final fragments. "'. . . *crafh of countleff breaking black illowf* . . . *high vein of gold* . . .'"

"I don't get it," Joe muttered. "Were there ever veins of gold in this area?"

Frank offered to find out. He went into the hall, where Joe heard him talking on the phone with Chet. Presently Frank returned, excited.

"Joe! I think I may have it!"

"What?"

"The answer to at least most of the message." Frank explained, "It figures that this fifth word from the end could be 'willows,' referring, in other words, to black willow trees. A hurricane would certainly cause many branches to 'break' and even whole trees to 'crash.' "

"Sure," Joe said, puzzled. "But if there were 'countless' black willows, they would be in an inland forest. I still don't see how any bottle could reach the sea from there."

Frank grinned. "I had a hunch and asked Chet to check it. Have you ever noticed where most black willows seem to grow?"

Joe recalled some of their past camping trips. "Near rivers or other bodies of water. Shadow Lake, and of course Willow River." Suddenly Joe caught the drift of Frank's reasoning. "Willow River, of course. That would account for Elias Dodd's message reaching the sea!"

Frank said thoughtfully, "And gold is often found in stream beds."

Neither of the brothers recognized the crude drawing of the leaf. "Chet may be able to identify it," Frank said.

Joe suggested that they check in town about past gold mines or claims to any in Bayport history.

"Good idea," Frank agreed. "Now for the big question—is this message a copy of the *real* one?"

"Any ideas about who brought it?" Joe asked.

"One," Frank answered. "Professor Martin Dodd, though I don't understand why he wouldn't identify himself."

Joe remembered their last meeting with Jack and his father. "Mr. Dodd did suggest there was an urgency about solving the Pilgrim mystery. Let's start treasure sleuthing early tomorrow."

Mrs. Hardy brought the morning mail to the breakfast table next day. The brothers received more letters of complaint from Bayport residents, but the last letter Joe opened had a Bridgewater postmark. He paled as he read it.

"Look at this!" he exclaimed, passing the typed letter to Frank. It said:

Hardys—You were suckers to back us. Don't meddle any more.

"It's signed '*Jack*'!" Frank cried out.

After the initial shock caused by the note, Frank became suspicious. "This doesn't sound like Jack. Did you save that grenade note? This typing looks the same."

The boys went upstairs and Joe produced the paper. He followed his brother into Mr. Hardy's study, where Frank got out a file on typewriter clues.

"I'm convinced of it!" he said at last. "Certain information here points to one interesting fact— both *were* typed by the same person. Also, the letters typed by the left hand are much darker—"

"Which might mean," Joe broke in, "that the person is—or was—left-handed. Slagel!"

After marking on the map the streams running into Willow River, Frank and Joe picked up Chet

at the Bayport Museum. Still tired from yesterday's trek and overland chase, Chet was nevertheless proud about his part in the black-willow
clue. He agreed to be their lookout for a plant like
that in the drawing.

The boys' plan was to cover certain areas daily
in their search for the treasure. Right now they
would sleuth in a region north of Route 7, keeping
a lookout for willow groves. The only stream in
the region, shaded by old black willows, offered no
clues to any gold or buried treasure and Chet saw
no plants matching the leaf sketch.

"What's the next assignment?" Chet asked. He
pulled a small, wrapped raw cauliflower from his
pocket, took off the paper, and started to eat it.
"Ever try this?" he asked. "Very nourishing."

"It just so happens we have," Frank replied.
"What say we have our first stakeout tonight?"

"Here?" Chet asked, munching.

"No. Out at Springer Road."

"Why don't we make it an overnight?" Joe proposed. "In the meantime, we'll finish fixing our
motorcycle radio."

The others liked the idea. After supper the
three assembled packs and drove out to Springer
Road. The boys set up a three-man shift among
some trees. The night passed slowly as the Hardys
and Chet each took a turn watching the night traffic for two hours, then sleeping during the next
four.

No thefts were reported over the radio, and the cars using the turnoff, which they logged by hour and description, were few and not suspect. An hour after sunrise on Saturday morning Frank woke the others and, disappointed, they headed home.

"You think maybe they've stopped stealing cars?" Chet yawned.

"I doubt it," Joe yelled back. "But there may have been a theft that hasn't been reported yet."

Joe's guess proved to be correct. Presently an announcement came over the police band that a car had been stolen several hours earlier outside a Shore Road gas station.

"That proves one thing," said Frank. "The thieves don't use Springer Road."

"One down, two to go!" Joe exulted. "Tonight we move to Route 7. Maybe we'll get a nibble on Mr. Slagel or his cronies."

Later that morning Joe called the Bayport Records Office for information about old gold claims.

"Any luck?" Frank asked as Joe hung up.

"Not yet. The only man who could tell us anything about mineral history in Bayport is out of town and won't be back until Monday."

That afternoon the Hardys met Chet to comb another area in their search for the Pilgrim treasure. Chet, in khaki shorts and a pith helmet, looked like an overstuffed safari guide. They hunted through several thickets and a stream bed near a farm owned by John Apperson, but found no trace of gold.

"We've hardly seen a willow twig all day," Chet moaned disconsolately as they sat on a rock to rest. He picked a burr out of his sneakers. "And I haven't spotted any plant with a leaf like in that drawing. Might as well look for a pine needle in a haystack."

"Still," said Frank, "with what we covered today, we can eliminate a lot of that shadowed area on our map."

Suddenly Joe had an idea and hopped down.

"A bird's-eye view of this whole region might reveal some small streams not on any of our maps. Think we could get hold of Larry Dillon at the airfield?"

"He's usually free this late in the afternoon," Frank said. "Let's try him!"

The airport lay not far from their present location, and it took them less than half an hour to reach the field. They skirted the modern terminal and soon reached a smaller hangar where several single-engine aircraft stood poised about the taxiing area.

Sidestepping grease puddles, the boys entered the silver hangar and found Larry in a small, makeshift office. He was just getting into a leather flight jacket and greeted them warmly.

"Sure, I'll be glad to take you fellows around for a buzz!" The tall, crisp-voiced pilot smiled

He slapped Chet heartily on the back and winked at Frank and Joe. "What do you think—shall we charge him for extra freight? Chet, you look as if you're dressed for a jungle adventure!"

Chet grinned. "My outfit is just for solving mysteries—and the cause of science!"

They followed Larry across the field to a handsome red, high-wing craft. Moments later, they were airborne.

"Any place in particular?" Larry asked above the din of the motors as he banked away from the sun.

"North Bayport would be fine," Frank answered.

As they flew eastward, coastal breakers came into view far below. They looked like a white lace fringe in the gentle wind. While Chet held the map spread out on his lap, Frank and Joe gazed through binoculars.

"I'm sorry these windows don't give you a bigger view," the pilot remarked. "At least we have good visibility today."

"This beats feet any day," Chet remarked languidly. "There's Bayport already!"

When they reached the city nestled around the sprawling, horseshoe-shaped inlet, Frank had Larry fly northward. They strained to pick up traces of small streams or ponds not on the map. Seeing none, they turned south, circling several times before reversing direction again.

"I guess the map is accurate," Frank said, after they had failed to uncover anything not charted. "Have you seen a spot that could be a hideout, Joe?"

"No. Every building looks accounted for on the map." Chet supported Joe's observation.

"Could we go down a little lower, Larry, for a couple of final spins?"

"Roger! Hold on!"

The plane nosed gracefully to a course nearer the ground. The black highway loomed larger, dotted with late-afternoon traffic. The shadow of their plane flickered on the surface of the blue sea.

They had just whined into a wide turn and started southward again, when they heard a ring of ripping steel to their rear. It was followed by a thudding flash of light inches away, and the shatter of glass in the instrument panel.

"We're being shot at!" Frank cried out.

"Keep away from the windows!" Larry yelled. He climbed frantically to a higher altitude.

"Good night!" Joe said, stunned. "Are we hit badly, Larry?"

"The motor's choking—I'm taking her back!"

As they pulled westward from the Shore Road area, the boys peered from the windows again, trying to determine the source of the bullets. But the altitude was too great.

Larry landed the plane safely. When investigators from the Civil Aeronautics Board arrived, the Hardys were looking at one of the slugs in the fuselage.

"They're from a submachine gun of foreign manufacture," one of the men reported.

Frank whispered to Joe, "That dud grenade was foreign made too! Makes me think of Dad's case."

The Hardys apologized to Larry for the trouble they had caused. "Nonsense." He smiled, wiping grease off his T-shirt. "I'll let you know if we get any leads to the sniper."

The boys rode to the Hardy home. There was no news of the missing Dodds or of the recently stolen cars.

Chet stayed to supper but proudly partook only of Mrs. Hardy's cooked vegetables. Aunt Gertrude stared incredulously, but offered him no dessert.

Later, Chet borrowed an old shirt and dungarees from Frank for the night's watch on Shore Road. After reassembling their gear they drove out to Route 7, the turnoff four miles south of Springer Road. The boys stationed themselves on a pine slope some fifty yards down the turnoff.

"We'll have to be on our toes tonight, men," Frank said. "There's more traffic on Route 7 than on Springer or Pembroke."

As darkness fell, the three arranged their shifts for the night. Joe propped up a twig fork-support for the binoculars while his brother stationed their motorcycles. Chet, who was to have the third shift, settled down on his sleeping bag with a small flash-light, engrossed in a thick book on botany.

"You fellows are pretty lucky to have a botanist at your service," he boasted, then yawned.

"Boy, are you going to itch tomorrow!" said Joe, and pointed to where Chet's bag rested in a patch of poison ivy.

"Oh, all right, maybe I don't know *everything* about botany," Chet grumbled, dragging his gear to another spot.

Hours later Chet took his watch. He sat cross-legged before the field-glass tripod listening to the police calls and looking over the Hardys' log of the cars which had passed that night. Presently he heard a motor.

"Maybe this is it!" he thought as two headlight beams appeared. The next instant Chet saw the dark-colored sedan suddenly speed up and roar wildly toward him on Route 7. It swerved, caromed off a bush, and raced down the road.

The noise awakened Frank and Joe. "That may be our first bite!" Frank yelled. "Let's go!"

CHAPTER VIII

The Ring of Fire

IN seconds Frank and Joe had started their motor-cycles, the headlights cutting the darkness of the woods. Racing along, the boys could see the red taillights of the speeding sedan ahead.

"Anything come over the police band?" Joe shouted back to Chet.

"Nothing about a theft."

The gap diminished, and the boys realized the car was slowing down.

"Maybe he thinks we're the police," Frank called out.

But the sedan cut speed still more and began to make a U-turn. "He's coming back. Let's keep with him!" Frank urged.

The driver appeared to take no notice of their pursuit. The boys followed him back to the turn-off and then down Shore Road.

Joe called to Frank, "He's heading for Bay-port!"

Dropping back, the boys trailed the car through the quiet city streets until it drew up before the Excelsior Hotel in the waterfront area. The Hardys swung behind a parked truck.

Frank motioned for the binoculars. When Chet handed them over, Frank focused on the sedan's driver, a bald thick-set man. He still did not seem to notice the boys as he crossed the street and entered the hotel.

Frank flashed an excited look at the others. "I think we've finally found our man!"

"Slagel?" Joe guessed hopefully.

"That's right."

Chet spoke up. "No wonder no hotel day clerks recognized his picture—he works—or steals—at night!"

"I don't get it," Joe said. "If Slagel stole that car, would he park it right in Bayport? And why the U-turn back on Route 7?"

"Or why speed up suddenly when he made the turn off Shore Road?" Chet interrupted.

"I don't know," Frank said, "but I'm going in the hotel for a second. Joe, take down the license and description of the car."

Frank came out of the hotel a few minutes later and rejoined the boys.

"The night clerk knows Slagel under the alias of James Wright," he reported. "Apparently Slagel has kept these late hours since checking in two weeks ago."

"That's about when the Shore Road thefts began!" Chet exclaimed.

The Hardys felt they should go to police headquarters and report the episode.

While Joe watched the motorcycles, Frank and Chet ran up the steps to headquarters. But when they reappeared, they looked disappointed.

"A car was stolen all right, but not the one driven by Slagel."

"Crumb!" Joe muttered. "It looks as if we'll have to stick with the Route 7 turnoff. Still, do you think Slagel is connected with the theft in *some* way?"

Frank shrugged. "What gets me is the stolen car. The thief may have used Pembroke Road, but it's also possible we missed him in chasing Slagel."

The three boys rode back to the turnoff for their gear before dropping Chet at home and returning to their own house. They spent a quiet Sunday, their only detective work being to call headquarters, but there was no news about the Dodds or the car thieves.

After breakfast Monday morning the Hardys phoned Chet and promised to meet him and the girls later in the day for a swim off the *Sleuth,* the Hardys' sleek motorboat.

Then they rode into town, parked, and posted themselves in sight of the Excelsior Hotel. They did not have long to wait. Slagel, dressed in Army surplus trousers, boots, and a summer jacket emerged. He was carrying a cane in his left hand.

"He doesn't limp," Frank remarked. "Wonder why he carries a cane."

Slagel jumped into the black sedan and pull out. The Hardys followed on their motorcycles, and saw him come to a halt two blocks away before a paint store. He entered and soon emerged with cans of paint in either hand. After several trips, he had loaded some twenty gallons into the trunk. He had just slammed the trunk shut when he glanced back at the watching boys.

A chill went down Joe's back. "Think he knows we've been tailing him?"

"He sure doesn't act like it," said Frank.

Slagel went to a telephone booth on the curb, dialed, and spoke briefly. Presently he returned to his car and moved into the Bayport traffic.

"It looks like Shore Road again," Frank noted, as Slagel rounded Barmet Bay a little later.

Farther north, where the road curved inland and had pastureland on both sides, the traffic thinned. Slagel increased speed, but the Hardys kept him in sight. Suddenly a moving mass of brown and white appeared just ahead of them.

"Cattle!" Frank exclaimed.

He and Joe were forced to slow down as the cows were driven across the road toward a wide meadow on their left.

"We're really blocked," Joe shouted.

Fortunately, no fence separated the highway

from the meadow, and the boys were able to steer off the road. But by the time the cattle had crossed, Slagel's car had disappeared around a curve.

Then Frank saw the farmer who had driven the cattle across the road. He was the same short, white-haired man who had caused their spill a week before with his stalled truck.

Parking their vehicles, the Hardys approached him, but he spoke first. "What do you kids think yer doin'? If yer gonna ride wild, jest keep off my land—you mighta killed one o' my prize critters!"

Frank's eyes blazed. "This isn't an authorized cattle crossing—you should know better than to drive your herd across a major road without giving some kind of warning!"

Seeing no point in futher heated words, Frank turned from the irate farmer and the boys rode off.

On the way home they discussed their unsuccessful pursuit of Slagel. "At least," said Frank, "we know where he's staying. Maybe next time we'll have better luck."

Back home for lunch, the boys spoke to their mother and Aunt Gertrude about the farmer.

"A farm just south of Pembroke Road?" their aunt asked "Laura, wouldn't that be George Birnham?"

Yes," said Mrs. Hardy. "He has lived here a number of years."

"Do you know anything else about him?" Frank said.

"An odd man," Aunt Gertrude replied. "I believe his grandfather was given the land by a member of the Dodd family, though Birnham has never done very well with it. I gave him an order over the phone once. He sold me some half-rotten tomatoes, and I told him a thing or two!"

Out of curiosity Joe consulted the new telephone directory. "Frank! Birnham's name *is* in here—which means he lied about having no phone! Why?" Joe's eyes narrowed. "He's blocked us off two times. What if it wasn't coincidence—that there's some tie-in between him and Slagel?"

"Let's pay a visit to his farm tonight," Frank answered. "If Biff will team up with us, we can still watch Route 7 too. Have you the same hunch about Slagel's paint that I do?"

"If you mean it's for repainting stolen cars—yes," Joe replied. "And that does make the hideout north of here."

Suddenly Frank remembered the flecks of paint they had found near the car tracks in the woods. He phoned Chief Collig to learn the test results. The police were convinced they were from the stolen car and the tire prints also. "My men have rechecked the area where you boys found the paint chips but couldn't come up with anything more."

"How about the collision noises, Chief?"

"The police have heard them too—once when a patrol was on the tail of a stolen car. But that's not all. Do you know who the first victim of the auto thefts was?"

Frank tried to recall the papers two weeks back. "Wasn't it a farmer somewhere out on Shore—"

"A farmer named George Birnham!"

"Birnham!" Frank exclaimed. In view of the boys' latest suspicions, this seemed a strange twist!

That afternoon Frank and Joe took the Pilgrim clue with them and combed another patch of woods in the vicinity of Willow River.

It was three o'clock when they came upon a granite rock formation near a wooded slope. Nearby were several black willow trees.

"It looks as if somebody else has been sleuthing around here," Frank said. He pointed to traces of footprints and digging. "These were all made by one person."

The stone looked as if it had been there a long time. But it was too small to have afforded shelter or a whole family even three hundred years ago. Joe looked without success for traces of a gold vein.

"Let's take a look at Birnham's farm by daylight," Frank suggested, and they rode off.

After parking at some distance, the two cautiously made their way along the dirt road turning off to the farm. The road was just beyond the rise at which they had lost sight of Slagel's car that morning. At a distance they could see Birnham working in a field. But there was no sign of Slagel's car. The brothers returned to their motorcycles.

Frank, gazing ahead, suddenly cried out. Above the tips of a thick birch forest a couple of miles ahead, a circular formation of black smoke could be seen rising. "That looks like the start of a forest fire! We'd better find out and then report it!"

Swiftly the boys shot north toward the column of smoke. When they braked to a halt at the forest edge, a crackling sound reached their ears.

"It's a fire all right, and there may be a house and people in there!" Joe exclaimed.

The Hardys hopped off and ran into the woods. Soon billows of choking smoke swirled their way. Tying handkerchiefs over their noses, the boys hurried forward. A minute later they reached a clearing, circled by flames.

In the middle of the ring of fire a man lay unconscious!

"It's Scratch!" Joe cried out.

Instantly he and Frank leaped over singeing flames toward the helpless man!

CHAPTER IX

The Spider's Net

By the time Frank and Joe dived through the last patch of searing flame, licks of fire had almost reached Scratch's prone figure.

Joe tied his shirt over the drifter's face and pulled him up into a fireman's carry. With Frank holding the man's legs, the boys dashed back through the flames, not stopping until they were a hundred yards from the spreading conflagration.

To the Hardys' relief, fire fighters were arriving, and the woods echoed with heavy vehicles, sirens, and shouts.

The Hardys coughed violently for several minutes while slapping their smoking trousers. Scratch was just reviving as three state policemen approached.

"How did it happen?" one of them asked.

"We don't know," said Frank, and explained what they had seen.

Scratch sat up, blinking, and thanked the boys for his rescue. The officer turned to him. "Scratch have you been careless with one of your camp-fires?"

"No, sir," he said. "I heard a car in the woods hereabouts, and come to take a look. Next thing I knew, somebody put a funny-smellin' rag in front o' my face. After that, I don't remember."

The officer looked skeptically at Scratch, but the Hardys were startled. Liquid gas again! "This fire could have been planned," said Frank. "It was arranged in a perfect circle."

"I guess you're right," the officer conceded.

After the fire was out and the police completed a fruitless search for clues to the arsonist, the officers and firemen left. Forest rangers continued inspecting the scene.

Scratch drew the boys aside. "I owe you fellers my life." He smiled. "Least I kin do is tell you about the tre-*men*-dous spider I seen."

"Spider?"

"Yep, last night, leastwise, it looked like one." The drifter shivered. "Big enough to be a man, but it sure didn't move like one!"

"Sounds weird!" Joe said.

"Where did you see it, Scratch?" Frank asked.

"On a rock ledge down the road a piece. I was strollin' towards my camp when he crawled out o' sight. I never seen a human spider in a web!"

The Hardys, knowing that Scratch was apt to

exaggerate, did not take his story seriously. They did not want to hurt his feelings, so they pretended to be impressed.

"We've got to get going," said Joe. "Take care, Scratch."

When the boys came out to the highway, Joe glanced at his watch. "Jeepers! We promised to meet Chet and the girls for a swim half an hour ago!"

They whizzed off. At the dock where the *Sleuth* was berthed, they were met with reproving glances. Not only were they late, but disheveled.

"Promises, promises," purred Iola Morton, as Joe slunk down the ramp. Chet's slim, brunette sister had small features and twinkling eyes, and looked very pretty in an aqua-colored swimsuit.

"Frank Hardy, it's about time!" sang out another voice. Callie Shaw, a slim blonde in a red suit, gasped at the boys' sooty appearance.

Chet sat comfortably in the back of the boat, finishing a piece of watermelon. "Wow! You look like boiled frankfurters. Wrap yourselves in rolls, with a little mustard, and I'll break my diet!"

The others laughed, then Frank explained their delay. "We'll change and be right with you."

The brothers ran to a nearby bathhouse. Then they rejoined the others and started up the *Sleuth's* motor. The sleek blue-and-white craft moved swiftly out into the bay, its bow chopping through glistening breakers. Frank steered around the tip of the bay and headed the *Sleuth* north. They cast anchor near a small cove.

Chet had hit the water before the anchor. "Come on in!" he gurgled, surfacing with immense satisfaction.

Amidst jokes about a "salt bath," the sooty Hardys followed the girls overboard.

The bracing water refreshed them. After a rest in the motorboat, the five swimmers decided to go in again. They waited for a black fishing boat to pass. It anchored a short distance away. Then Callie dived in. Several seconds went by. She did not reappear.

"Something may have happened to Callie!" Iola said fearfully. The three boys dived in at once and plunged beneath the surface. Twenty feet down Frank's blood chilled. Callie, her face blanched with fear, was struggling violently.

She was enclosed in a small, tightly wound net!

His lungs bursting, Frank reached her, grasped the net, and started upward. When they broke surface, Callie was choking and too weak to swim. Desperately, Frank bore her to the *Sleuth*. Joe cut the nylon net and Callie was lifted over the side. She gestured that she was all right, but it was several minutes before she could explain what had happened.

"Some man—he was in a black skin-diving suit and mask—grabbed me and threw the net around . . ."

The sound of a motor reached their ears. The fishing boat nearby was heading away.

"He may have come from that boat!" said Frank. "Let's find out! There was a black fishing boat around just before the accident to Jack's boat!"

They pulled anchor and Frank steered the *Sleuth* after the fishing boat. The boys signaled to the pilot several times. He cut his engine as they drew alongside.

The fisherman, young and slim, wore a checkered sport shirt and a white yachting cap. He appeared annoyed at being disturbed.

"What do you want?" he asked curtly.

"Know anything about a skin diver around the cove back there?" Frank asked.

The young man started his motor. "Skin diver? No." His craft roared away.

Upset by the near-fatal accident to Callie, the five young people headed back to the boathouse. The Hardys bade good-by to Chet, Callie, and Iola, who planned to report the incident to the maritime authorities.

As the brothers were locking up, they saw Tony docking his *Napoli*. They related their recent adventures.

Tony whistled. "You've been busy! I'm out in the *Napoli* nearly every day, so I'll keep an eye on that fishing launch. It's sure suspicious why the pilot pulled away so fast. Also, if I see any-

Frank swam frantically toward the trapped girl!

thing of the Dodds' boat, I'll let you know."

On the way home, Frank and Joe stopped at the Records Building to check on past gold claims in the vicinity. The clerk who was familiar with the older mineral files was there. They spoke with him in a small office adjoining musty rows of books.

"Gold?" the white-haired man repeated, smiling agreeably. "Are you fellows hoping to strike it rich before school resumes?"

"No." Frank chuckled. "Our interest is historical. Have you any record of gold streaks at all—particularly north of Bayport?"

The old man shook his head. "No, son. To my knowledge, no gold has ever been found, or sought for that matter, within fifty miles of Bayport. But it's odd you should ask too. Another fellow was in here just a few hours ago looking for the same information. Didn't give his name."

"What did he look like?" Frank cut in.

The clerk removed his spectacles. "Maybe forty, or fifty, dark hair, a beard. Sounded like an educated fellow."

The boys thanked the clerk and drove home, wondering who the anonymous inquirer was. Someone who had knowledge of the Pilgrim clue? "The beard might have been a disguise," Joe remarked. "I doubt that the man was Slagel, though. He'd never strike anyone as being an educated person."

"The bearded man could be the missing professor—Martin Dodd!" Frank suggested.

Later, just before sunset, the boys were seated in Mr. Hardy's study reviewing their sleuthing plans for the evening. Suddenly Joe stood up. "Frank! Let's move our watch to Pembroke Road tonight!"

Frank knit his brows. "But we haven't eliminated Route 7 yet."

"I think we can!" Joe said. "There seems to be a pattern shaping up: the stolen car U-turns, the warning notes from the same person, Jack's things being found at theft scenes—whoever masterminds this operation has made an effort to throw the police off track. Well, what better way than to send Slagel around a turn—leaving skid marks—while someone else whisks the stolen car away to another spot, like Pembroke Road?"

"Joe, you're right! Decoy maneuvers! That might also account for the tire tracks and paint we found in the woods!"

The Hardys agreed on a plan to watch both the Birnham farm and Pembroke Road. By now it was dark, so after contacting Biff Hooper and Chet, they met them midway out on Shore Road. There they split up, Biff and Joe going farther north with the motorcycles to watch the intersection. Chet and Frank went in Chet's jalopy to George Birnham's farm.

The moon had risen, but was occasionally obscured by clouds. Frank guided Chet to a secluded woods. The jalopy was parked at the edge and the boys set out, carrying packs. Silently they walked across the dark farm fields where silvery mist gave the air a chill.

When the lights of Birnham's farmhouse appeared on the west side of Shore Road, they stopped. There was no place to hide, but Frank pointed to deep furrows in a field.

"We can lie low between those and get a pretty good view of anything going on near the house."

Chet followed Frank as he crawled under a wooden fence. The boys unrolled their sleeping bags between two rows of turned-up soil. Lying on their sides, they watched the house. Occasionally Frank glanced through his binoculars.

The hours passed slowly, uninterrupted except for the rhythmic chant of katydids and the boys' whispers, both of them having decided to keep awake until one became tired. Chet bit noisily into his last carrot.

"*Shhh!*" Frank whispered. "Birnham will think somebody's turned on that tractor I see over there!" Chet muffled his bites and laughter.

An hour later the boys saw a black sedan pull up the dirt road to the house. Frank watched through the binoculars. "It's Slagel!" he whispered excitedly as Birnham came out on the porch. "So those two are in cahoots! Wish we could hear what they're saying."

Presently Slagel returned to his car and drove out, heading south on the highway. Then the farmer left the porch and walked to the end of the dirt road. Frank and Chet saw the squat figure duck under the fence and cross the field some fifty feet to their rear. Fortunately, the moon had gone under again.

"Keep as low as you can!" Frank whispered.

He and Chet listened keenly. In a moment they heard a motor starting up. Frank stole a backward glance and saw Birnham seated atop the large tractor to which a cultivator was attached.

"What's he doing?" Chet asked, burrowing deeper into his sleeping bag.

Frank watched as the noisy vehicle began to move. The farmer did not turn on the headlights.

"He's heading in our direction!" Frank gasped.

He could feel Chet shaking violently alongside him. "Quick!" said Frank. "Keep low and roll to the right!"

Chet struggled to obey, but his eyes bulged with desperation. "I can't—the zipper on my sleeping bag is stuck!"

Frank yanked wildly at the zipper, but it was no use!

CHAPTER X

Strange Roadblock

MUFFLING Chet's yell, Frank rolled him violently over and landed quickly on top of him. The tractor and its whirling blades missed them by inches!

The vehicle's sound grew fainter as Birnham continued ahead. As Frank looked up he noticed a large truck passing slowly on the road going in the direction of Bayport.

"It's okay, pal," he said, patting Chet. "But let's get to the road before Birnham starts back on *this* row!"

Chet finally freed himself from the sleeping bag. Trailing it behind him, the heavy youth followed Frank across the field, running in a low crouch. Once beneath the fence, the boys paused to catch their breath, and saw Birnham turn.

"I've had it," Chet moaned softly. "Let's get out of here!"

"Shhh!"

Puzzled by the farmer's strange activity, they watched his tractor, still without lights, churn earth at a rise near the highway. After twenty minutes, the vehicle stopped. Birnham cut the motor, jumped down, and returned to his house. In a few moments the building was dark.

"What was that all about?" Chet asked. "Did Birnham know we were here and do that just to scare us?"

"If not, why this night work without lights?" said Frank.

Chet grimaced. "Nuttiest thing I've ever seen!"

Exhausted, the two boys took shifts for the remainder of the night. When nothing more had transpired by sunrise, they drove north and rejoined Joe and Biff.

They had had an uneventful night at Pembroke Road but were excited by Frank and Chet's adventure, and agreed that Birnham's actions were indeed suspicious.

Frank asked, "Did you pick up anything on the radio?"

"Nothing new," Biff said.

He climbed into Chet's jalopy and they roared off. The brothers soon passed them on the motorcycles. The Hardys were just entering Bayport when report of a theft came over the police band.

". . . the car, reported missing at Lucas Street in Bridgewater was later recovered, abandoned on

the other side of town. Owner, while sitting in his parked car, was gassed. No clues . . ."

"In Bridgewater!" Joe exclaimed. "That's not only the first theft someplace besides Shore Road, but the first time the thieves have failed! Apparently they were frightened off before they could get out of town."

"So it was the car thieves who gassed Scratch and us," said Frank. Another idea struck him. "Bridgewater's at the end of Pembroke Road, Joe—also, remember it's the postmark on that phony typed note from Jack!"

"Come on! Let's check on Slagel at the Excelsior!"

The Hardys cycled to the waterfront hotel, and Joe went in to inquire. When he emerged from the run-down doorway, his expression was not happy. "Slagel—or 'James Wright'—checked out early this morning!"

The boys decided to sacrifice their treasure hunt for the day and check the hotels in Bridgewater for Slagel. First they stopped at a diner and had a quick breakfast. Afterward, they hurried to their motorcycles and started up. Just then a middle-aged man strode over to them.

"You're the Hardy boys, aren't you?" he demanded.

They nodded. "My car was stolen a week ago!" he shouted. "You and your father had a nerve giving bail money to car thieves and allowing them to escape! What are you doing to help? If my car is not recovered, I'll hold you personally responsible!" The man stormed away.

Frank was depressed. "This feeling in town worries me, Joe—not because of the ridicule or threats, but because so many people seem to be convinced that the Dodds are guilty."

As the Hardys coasted to the corner, Joe groaned. Approaching them with a broad smirk was the dumpy figure of would-be detective Oscar Smuff.

"What ho, it's our two young sleuths!" he sang out flatly. "Any sign of your Dodd friends, the car thieves?"

Frank was too accustomed to Smuff's ways to be incensed. "We think the Dodds are innocent," he responded.

"If you boys were smart," Smuff went on, "you'd memorize features of all the stolen cars, like I do. I'm watching the streets."

"For the Dodds too?" Joe asked.

Smuff nodded smugly. "Or accomplices. I think a woman is involved in the racket somewhere, and if my deductions are correct, she's got blond hair."

He whipped out a note pad and glanced at a scribbled list. Then the "detective" looked up at a sedan stopping for a red light. Suddenly his eyes widened. "There's one of the stolen cars now!"

Frank recognized the blond woman driver as

Chief Collig's wife and tried to restrain Smuff. But the self-appointed detective excitedly darted into the street and up to the sedan. Poking his head in the window, he started to accuse the woman loudly. She turned to face him indignantly.

The next moment Smuff stepped back, open-mouthed and flaming with embarrassment as he realized his mistake. By this time the light had changed and horns were blasting impatiently. Stuttering apologies, Smuff retreated rapidly, wiping his forehead. Mrs. Collig drove off and the deflated detective hastily returned to the sidewalk. He passed the grinning Hardys with a sheepish look and disappeared around a corner.

Still chuckling, Frank and Joe rode off. They passed the Birnham farm and turned down Pembroke Road on the way to Bridgewater.

"Everything seems to narrow down to this road—and now to Bridgewater," Frank remarked. "And according to the map—some of Birnham's property touches Pembroke."

As the brothers passed an open field, they noticed a man ahead leaning comfortably on a fence. He held a walking stick in one hand.

"Slagel!" Joe exclaimed.

"It's time we had a word with him!" Frank declared.

The Hardys rolled to a stop, hopped off, and

hurried toward Slagel. He turned as if to walk
away, but the boys confronted him.

"Mr. Wright—?" Frank began.

The broad-nosed, bald man wiped his sleeve
across his face, drumming a cane on the fence.
"What of it?" he drawled.

"We understand you worked for a Mr. Dodd—
that is, when your name was Slagel."

The man's lips tightened. "It's none of your
business what I do!"

"Maybe not," Frank said. "We just thought you
might be able to give us a clue to where the Dodds
might be." He noticed Slagel's expression change
to a supercilious smile.

" 'Fraid I can't help you there," said Slagel,
leaning back. "Besides, why should I bother
spendin' my time here with car-thief bailers. Anyway, I'm doin' work for Birnham now."

"Like stealing cars?" Joe interjected.

Slagel's face flushed. He leaned down and
swung the end off his cane. *A long silver blade
pointed at Joe's face!*

"Beat it!" Slagel rasped viciously. "You're tres-
passin' on private property!"

More surprised than awed by the lethal sword,
Joe looked at Frank. At his brother's signal, they
walked back to their motorcycles. Slagel was still
glaring lividly at them as they rode off in the
direction of Bridgewater.

"At least we shook him up a bit." Frank smiled. "Even if we can't find out where he's staying, we know for sure he's in league with Birnham—and not just for farm work. That sword cane didn't look very innocent."

"But good for puncturing tires!" Joe added, remembering the flats reported on some cars near the stolen ones.

In Bridgewater the brothers stopped at a drugstore, had lunch, then purchased a town map which also had a list of the hotels in the immediate area. They were fewer in number than those in Bayport. The Hardys checked all but two in an hour. At this point, they entered one at the east end of town. The desk clerk immediately recognized Slagel's picture.

"Yes, he checked in today. Name of Wright. He just dropped his things off, then asked directions to the telegraph office."

Frank and Joe headed for the office a block away. Inside, a woman behind a typewriter affirmed the fact that a Slagel had sent a message out, though she was not permitted to divulge its contents.

As the boys walked away, Frank said, "Joe, sometimes when a person sends a telegram, he makes a draft of it first." He saw a wastebasket beneath a writing counter and hurried over. It took him only a second to find a torn piece of yellow paper with Slagel's name at the bottom. When he found the second half, the boys left the office excitedly. Outside, they pieced the halves together and read the message:

> MORE NERVE NOW. TRYING FOR 8-CYL-
> INDER STOCK. TAKING CARE OF TWO
> FRIENDS. ATTEND TO THEM WHEN JOB
> DONE IN WEEK OR SO. EXPECT YOU FOR
> SHIPMENT TOMORROW.

The message was addressed to Carlton Melliman in New York City.

"Carlton Melliman—C. M.," Joe mused. "Frank! He must be our mysterious visitor who wouldn't give his name. And the '8-cylinder' business—that cinches Slagel's connection with the Shore Road gang!"

Frank nodded. "It fits. I wonder how Melliman figures in. 'Two friends' might refer to Mr. Dodd and Jack, which gives us only a week before— We're going to have to work fast!"

"If we only knew what this 'shipment' is and where it's going," Joe murmured.

The Hardys stopped at an outside phone booth and Frank dialed his home. Mrs. Hardy answered. "I'm glad you called," she said. "Your father phoned a little while ago, and gave me a list of things for you boys to look up in his file—information to help him on his case. He's going to call back tonight at ten for your data."

"We're on our way," Frank assured her.

When they reached home, the brothers washed and changed, then started work. Among the items their father had requested were the first dates of manufacture of various foreign weapons and ammunition, as well as serial numbers for certain guns made abroad.

The job took most of the afternoon. The boys had almost finished when Frank exclaimed, "Joe! Remember? The grenade and those machine-gun bullets were of foreign make."

"Sure enough! You think they have a connection with Dad's arms-smuggling case?"

"Possibly, since we're pretty sure they were used by thieves."

After supper Frank and Joe handed Mrs. Hardy the data they had compiled and asked her to relay it to their father. "We'll get back to our case now, Mother," Joe explained. "Please give Dad our regards."

The boys had decided to cycle along Pembroke Road. Seeing nothing suspicious, they returned to Shore Road. As they approached the intersection, the sun was setting. There was no traffic.

"Let's cruise south," Frank proposed.

"Right."

The young sleuths turned onto Shore Road, with Joe in the lead. Some distance along they had reached a section of the road with a sheer drop to the left and a steep rocky formation on their right, when Joe happened to glance back out to sea. He gave a start, then beckoned Frank to turn around. When they were facing north, Joe pointed toward a high shadowed rock cliff that dropped to the ocean.

A spidery figure was moving slowly up the rock face!

The boys rode forward to get a closer look. A turn in the road made them lose sight of the figure. When their view was unobstructed, the spidery form had vanished! They watched the rock cliff a few minutes but saw nothing in the twilight.

"I'll bet that was the spider Scratch told us about," Joe declared.

"He looked half human, half spider," Frank remarked. "I'd sure like to know where he went. Well, let's go. It'll be dark soon."

Frank turned around and went ahead, increasing speed, and snapped on his head lamp. Presently he noticed a slight glitter over the center of the highway. As the reflection grew nearer, alarm coursed through his body.

Strung chest-high across the entire highway was a fine steel-wire net!

It was too late to stop. Frank ducked and closed his eyes, yelling as loudly as he could at the same time. *"Joe, look out!"*

CHAPTER XI

Guard on the Cliff

FRANK swerved to safety an instant before his brother's motorcycle crashed into the glistening wire. Joe flew into the air, as his vehicle twisted and smashed into a tree to which the net was tied.

"Joe!" cried Frank, leaping off his cycle and running to the still form in the roadway. Joe lay unconscious, blood oozing from his head.

Both of Joe's legs were badly bruised, and Frank feared he might have suffered a concussion. Frantically Frank waved down an oncoming car. The driver offered to take Joe to Bayport Hospital. Frank followed on his motorcycle. Joe's motorcycle lay in a tangled heap of gray steel and chrome.

An hour later Frank, Mrs. Hardy, and Aunt Gertrude stood at Joe's bedside in the hospital. A physician watched Joe as he mumbled, moving his head slightly.

"He has had a nasty shock, but he should be coming out of it soon," he reassured the others before stepping quietly from the room. "Just see that Joe gets plenty of rest in the next few days."

After spending the night at the hospital, Joe was moved home. He had a slight limp and wore a large bandage on his head.

"How do you feel, partner?" Frank asked, as Joe rested on the living-room couch.

"A little weak." He grinned. "But still in one piece. Who put up that wire?"

"I wish I knew, Joe, but my guess is it was the work of the car thieves. They had the wire netting ready to string across the road."

"Was there another theft?" Joe asked.

"Yes. This time they copped one from the Ely estate during a dinner party."

"The Ely estate! Why, that place is walled in like a fortress!"

"Right. Those thieves are bold, all right. Joe, that barrier across the road reminds me of the nylon net Callie was trapped in underwater. I have a hunch one of the thieves is a skin diver."

Joe whistled, then grinned. "You don't think the thieves hide the stolen cars under water!"

Frank laughed. "It would be a good place! Maybe that spider-man owns an underwater garage!"

At that moment Mrs. Hardy and Aunt Gertrude came into the room, dressed to go shopping.

"Joe, promise me you'll rest," his mother said,

her face much brighter than it had been the night before.

"Except for this limp," he said, smiling, "I feel as if I could run ten laps!"

"Don't you dare, Joe Hardy!" Aunt Gertrude scolded.

The two women had been gone half an hour when the boys heard the front door open and a familiar voice call, "Hello! Where is Joe?"

"Dad!"

Fenton Hardy strode with concern into the living room, his face relaxing when he saw Joe sitting up. After shaking hands warmly with his sons, he asked, "You all right, Joe? Mother phoned me about your accident."

"I'm okay, Dad." Joe grinned.

The brothers briefed their father on what had happened to date in the mystery. When they mentioned liquid gas, the foreign grenade, and machine-gun bullets, he started to say something, then changed his mind.

"I have some hunches. If I'm right—" He stopped. "It's my opinion you're up against a highly professional operation. Promise me you'll be careful, for the Dodds' sake as well as yours."

"How about your own case, Dad?" Frank asked.

"I'll be doing some risky undercover work in the next day or so. Sorry I can't tell you about it now, but you can reach me at the usual New York address. Meanwhile, you boys use the family car. I understand your motorcycle, Joe, is a wreck."

Frank drove his father to the airport and came home for a light salad lunch. Mrs. Hardy apologized for the wilted lettuce. "Apparently a different farmer is supplying stores in town since the Dodds' disappearance."

Later, Joe persuaded his mother to let the boys go out in the *Sleuth,* promising he would be quiet. At the Prito boathouse they noticed that Tony's boat was not in dock.

"If we can find Tony, he may have some leads on that strange fisherman in the black boat," Frank said, and drove on to the Hardy boathouse.

"I'll take the wheel," Joe volunteered. "That won't hurt my legs."

The *Sleuth's* powerful engine droned smoothly as they cruised south to Willow Beach. Then they turned back across Barmet Bay and north.

Just past Beacon Point the boys caught sight of the *Napoli.* Waving to Tony, they drew alongside.

"Wow! What did Iola do to you?" Tony asked, looking at the bandage on Joe's head.

"Somebody handed me a line," Joe quipped, as Frank laughed. The Hardys told Tony of the accident. He asked several questions but seemed eager to tell them something himself.

"Would you guys believe me if I told you I saw a—a huge spider—out here last night?"

Tony described a black form scampering into a crevice in a rock cliff farther up the coast.

Frank started. "We saw one too. Where exactly did *you* see the spider?"

Tony paused in thought. "On a cliff just south of that big seaside estate."

"The Ely estate!" Joe exclaimed excitedly. "Frank, it was on that same cliff that we saw the spider-man!"

The Hardys mentioned the theft which had taken place at the estate the previous night and wondered what relation the "spider" could have to it.

"That's not all," Tony continued. "I've been watching our fisherman friend—the one you told me about. Apparently he does some of his fishing at night. Sometimes he has one lamp on his boat, other times two. He keeps on the move up and down the coast."

"Is he fishing?" Frank asked.

"I guess so, or else trolling. I didn't want him to catch on that I was watching and kept the *Napoli* at some distance."

In the *Sleuth* the Hardys followed the *Napoli* north along the coast to the place where Tony had seen the "spider." The ocean washed at the foot of a high rock cliff, atop which the Ely estate could be seen. The boys glided beneath an overhanging ledge.

"It'd take a skilled climber to scale that and steal a car," Frank remarked, training his field glasses up the sheer wall.

Joe, meanwhile, noticed a gossamer-like pattern in the water. "Look, fellows!"

The three boys stared at the ghostly, weblike rope floating in the waves. With a pole, Frank pulled it aboard.

"It's rope netting, probably for climbing!" Frank exclaimed. "I have a hunch our spider-man is an accomplished climber—"

"And car thief!" Joe finished. "He could easily —at dusk—look like a spider."

"But still," Tony put in, "that can't account for the daylight thefts. Anybody swimming in or climbing a precipice like this would be seen."

Tony said he had also discovered that the fisherman moored at a small inlet to the north along the coast. The *Napoli* and the *Sleuth* sped to the area.

A makeshift dock extended from a narrow crescent of sand at the base of a high bluff with a "No Trespassing" sign nailed to it. Several buoys dotted the water out from the shore.

As Frank gazed at the peaceful scene, he wondered: Could stolen cars be shipped out by sea from this beach? The possibility seemed unlikely Not only was the water cluttered with buoys, but the only grassy slope leading down to the beach was too steep for cars to descend.

The two boats ran farther up the coast. Frank gazed at the shore through binoculars. Seeing nothing suspicious, they turned back.

They were passing along the fisherman's secluded beach when Joe's hands tensed on the wheel at an eerie sound. Something had scraped against the *Sleuth's* bottom!

"I'm going overboard to take a look!" Frank said. He stripped to his shorts, kicked off his shoes, and dived in.

The scraping sound had stopped by the time Frank was under water and he found no sign of any rocks beneath the craft. Another thought occurred to him. Had somebody intended to sabotage the *Sleuth* as he had Jack's boat? Frank could find no evidence of this on the bottom of the *Sleuth*.

Climbing back into the boat, he reported this fact, then suggested they move along the coast for more sleuthing.

As they left the area, Frank watched the coast through binoculars. Suddenly he said, "Joe! Slow down! I want to get a better look at the top of that bluff!"

Through the two eyepieces, he could see a lone figure peering, through similar glasses, at the boys. As the man removed his binoculars before disappearing into the brush, Frank's recognition was instant.

Carlton Melliman!

CHAPTER XII

Planted Evidence?

"MELLIMAN!" Joe exclaimed.

The boys told Tony of their visit from the unctuous New York businessman.

"I wish we could trail him," said Frank. "But we'd never catch him."

"On whose property is that bluff?" Tony asked.

Joe referred to a map. "According to this, that beach is part of Birnham's property! He owns land on both sides of Shore Road."

As Frank headed back to the Bayport dock area, he said, "Slagel, Birnham, a spider-man, and now Melliman—they're like pieces in a jigsaw puzzle. But I think we're at least fitting some of them into place."

Back in their crime lab, the brothers discussed the latest leads in the mystery.

"We must find out where the shipment mentioned in the telegram is to take place," Frank declared. "It must be a load of stolen cars."

Joe suggested the possibility of the cars being moved out of the Bayport area by truck.

"I'm thinking of Birnham's covered produce job that blocked us. It's big enough to carry two cars at a time."

Suddenly an idea came to Frank. "When Chet and I had that narrow squeak with Birnham's tractor I noticed a truck—maybe Birnham's—heading south on Shore Road past us."

"Let's call Chief Collig and suggest his patrols take a look inside the truck."

"Good idea."

The Bayport chief proved reluctant at first to conduct the search, largely because the farmer himself had been the first victim of the automobile thieves. But at length he promised to do so.

Collig mentioned that the police, too, were being flooded by letters of protest over the continuing thefts. Another car had been stolen—and recovered—in Bridgewater that morning.

"Jack Dodd's identification bracelet was found under the front seat," he added.

"Planted, of course," said Joe. "The poor guy."

"We're inclined to agree," Collig said. "We're running twenty-four-hour patrols, and, with the Bridgewater department, several roadblocks. I hope we'll have some word on your friends or their uncle soon."

But when the chief called after receiving reports from his men, the result was a disappointment to the boys. The Birnham truck, returning from Bayport to the farm, had been halted but only empty crates had been found inside.

By suppertime Joe said he was completely recovered and suggested that they watch Pembroke Road that night.

"Joe," said Frank, "remember your idea about the gang's decoy tactics? We may be up against the same trick at Pembroke. The postmark on that last note, tire marks near Pembroke, maybe even Slagel's moving to Bridgewater—it's just too pat. A couple of those thefts could be phonies to draw the police and us away from Shore Road!"

Joe agreed, and they decided to watch only the farm that night. The boys wired their father in code about the net and Melliman, then changed into fresh sport clothes and telephoned Chet they wanted him along. They picked him up in Mr. Hardy's car, and stationed themselves beyond a rise in the road. From there they had a better view of the dirt lane leading to Birnham's farm.

Shortly after midnight, it began to rain, and the boys shivered under wet ponchos for four hours. Finally, having spotted nothing suspicious, they returned to the car and drove back toward Bayport. Chet looked longingly at an open frankfurter stand as they passed it.

"How's the diet?" Joe asked. "You've lost weight. But it'll be a phenomenon when one Chester Morton loses his appetite!"

"My spirits, not my appetite are dampened," Chet chattered, as he huddled in the back seat with a large box of raisins. "Do you th-think Birnham, Slagel and Company are l-laying l-low for a wh-while?"

"Could be," Frank said. "They may have found out we weren't at Pembroke Road tonight. Not knowing where we were, they decided to play safe."

The sun had not yet risen as they passed the vacant Dodd farmhouse silhouetted ominously against the dawn sky.

"Frank, somebody's inside the house! I just saw a light flicker in an upstairs window!"

Applying the brakes, Frank reversed direction and drove as silently as possible down the farm road. Chet seemed disposed to stay locked inside the car but finally accompanied the others quietly around to the backyard. Above the shadowed screen porch, a slight glow was visible in Jack's second-floor bedroom.

The back door was locked. Joe tried a window. "It's open!" he whispered. He noticed Chet trembling. The stout youth swallowed.

"I'm n-not scared. Just c-cold!"

Joe preceded the others through the window, where they paused and listened. They heard the faint thump of footsteps overhead.

"Careful!" Frank whispered.

Tiptoeing, he led the way through the kitchen.

They had just reached the foot of the stairs when Chet sneezed. Both Hardys winced as the raucous sound echoed through the house. The footsteps above stopped for a moment, then resumed at a rapid pace. Soon they ceased altogether. There was only silence.

Flushing and gesturing apologetically, Chet followed the brothers hurriedly up the stairs into the darkness of the hallway. Motioning Joe to guard the stairway, Frank played his flashlight into Jack Dodd's abandoned room. When the beam touched a half-open drawer, he flipped on the wall switch.

The room was empty. Frank crept down the carpeted hall, searching one by one three other rooms before returning with a shrug to the others.

Chet, his face pale with fear, was the first to break the silence. "N-nobody here. Let's go!" He started for the stairs but was beckoned back.

While Frank beamed his flashlight down the stairs to spot anyone coming up, Joe and Chet looked around Jack's room. Except for the open drawer, there seemed to be no disorder. Joe was about to open the closet door when Frank called out in a loud voice:

"I guess nobody's up here. Let's head back to the *vein of gold.*"

Sensing his brother's strategy of flushing out anyone inside the closet, Joe led Chet to the hall. Turning off the lights, the three boys walked downstairs. They had just turned toward the kitchen when a deep voice came from the top of the steps.

"Excuse me, are you the Hardy boys?"

Both brothers' flashlight beams revealed a mustached man dressed in slacks and a navy-blue hooded sweater.

Joe, starting cautiously up, answered, "Yes. Are you—"

"Martin Dodd." The man smiled. Turning on the lights, he came down and shook hands cordially with each of the boys. "I'm sorry about the cloak-and-dagger game, but I had to be careful."

There was no doubt but that the tall, middle-aged man was the professor whose picture they had seen. He led them to a small den in the rear of the house.

"When I got word of my brother's and nephew's arrests, I knew somebody had plotted against them. I could have gone to the police but thought I might be able to find them by working under-cover. And also," he added, "because a private mystery is involved. Moreover, I didn't want any publicity because of my position at the college."

"Then it *was* you who left the Pilgrim clue at our house!" Frank said.

"That's right. I hoped to get your father's help, but finding he was away, I decided to leave you the clue in the hope that—separately—you two or I might hit upon its solution. I couldn't chance your giving me away to the police."

The energetic professor agreed that his relatives had been victims either of an accident or a kidnapping, though he failed to see how news of the lost Pilgrim treasure could have reached other ears. Of the Shore Road thefts, or Slagel or Birnham, he knew little.

"Then you didn't reach Bayport until after your relatives had disappeared?" Chet asked.

"No. I heard the news over the radio. It was then that I decided to leave my car in another town and camp in the northern Bayport area. With authorities already dragneting the region for my relatives, it seemed best for me to work from the Pilgrim-clue angle. While I've had little success in decoding it yet, I feel strongly that something may have happened to them while tracking down—or being forced to track down—the clue."

As Martin Dodd spoke, a cordial relationship began to develop between the boys and the astronomy professor.

He went on, "Jack had written to me about trying to get your help on our mystery, but I didn't know you and wanted to be extra careful." The professor smiled. "That is why I watched you several times when I heard your voices in the woods."

"Then it was your footprints we spotted," said Frank, "and you who inquired about the gold in Bayport."

Dodd nodded. "I've used a disguise whenever I

went into town. I wish you and I had had more success with the black-willow clue or the plant drawing."

Martin Dodd told the boys he was interested in astronomy and carried telescopic equipment on his trips. He now unfolded a small piece of paper and handed it to Frank. It was a photostat of a note in the same handwriting as that in the Pilgrim clue, except that it contained several numbers, angles, estimations, and the words: "*the evening ftar crefcent.*"

"I owe you boys an apology," the professor said. "I didn't give you this, which is also part of Elias Dodd's last message, and refers to the position of the planet Venus in the late summer of 1647."

"Which might help locate the treasure site?"

"Yes. Elias Dodd attempted, before dying, to cite his position relative to that of Venus. If his estimation was accurate, it may indeed pinpoint the location." The professor paused. "I believe I am on the verge of solving these calculations, which seem to be leading me farther east each day."

Chet mulled over the piece of paper. "These sure are complicated numbers!"

"That is why I didn't include them with the rest of the message," Martin Dodd replied. "The fact that he called Venus the 'evening star' indicates its crescent was in a period of eastern elongation.

As you may know, the motions of Venus are irregular, with identical phases for a given month recurring only about every eight years."

"Then there *is* a deadline for solving the Pilgrim mystery!" Frank exclaimed.

"That's right, Frank, and time is running out, since this particular phase of Venus won't be seen in August again for another eight years. Boys, the progress you've made so far astonishes me. I think by working together we may find the treasure, but more important, my brother and nephew before it is too late."

"Let's meet early tomorrow afternoon," said Frank. "We'll come here."

"Very good."

On the way home Chet dozed in the back seat. When they arrived at his farm, he asked, "What's hatching, guys?"

"Some work for you. Game?" Joe said.

Chet was cagey. "Tell me first."

"Will you try to follow Birnham's truck on its rounds today? It's big and red."

"Oh, sure," Chet agreed.

The Hardys arrived home to find a hearty breakfast awaiting them. As they ate, the brothers discussed the purchase in Harpertown of a used car as part of a plan for solving the case. "I'll go," Frank offered.

Joe remained at home and greeted Chet when

he stopped in before his reconnaissance errand.

"Chet! You look starved!" Aunt Gertrude observed.

"Suppose so." He yawned. "Do feel kind of empty. But no food, thanks. I've decided I'm not so interested in land vegetation any more."

"You mean you're going to break your diet?" Joe asked.

"Certainly not! But I think I'll become an algologist."

"An algologist?"

Chet brandished a green book with a picture of the ocean on its cover. "Algology is the study of marine vegetation—seaweed and stuff."

Joe grinned. "By this time next year you'll be a poor fish?" Chet gave his friend a black look.

At that moment the mail arrived. One letter was addressed to the Hardy Boys. Joe showed the envelope to Chet. "Another Bridgewater postmark." Quickly he tore it open to find a handwritten message:

> Frank and Joe—Jack and I have escaped criminals. We want to give ourselves up but not before talking with you. Meet us alone beneath Saucer Rock on Pine Road at 12 P.M. today. Please be there!

CHAPTER XIII

A Hungry Sleuth

"Do you think the message is another trick?" Chet asked as Joe studied the note.

"Could be. The handwriting's not Jack's, but it could be Mr. Dodd's. What do you think?"

Chet shrugged. "It *sounds* like Mr. Dodd, but I still think it's suspicious. You're not going to go, are you?"

Joe paced the room. "If only Frank were here!" He looked at his watch. "It's almost noon now! That doesn't give us much time to decide!"

At last he made up his mind to go to the rendezvous. "I can't afford *not* to go—I wouldn't sleep tonight if I just dismissed the possibility that the Dodds really may have escaped. There isn't time to check the handwriting. Keep your fingers crossed. If you don't hear from me by four, get out to Saucer Rock with Frank as fast as possible! Meanwhile, good luck in town and don't let Birnham's driver see that you're tailing him!"

After seeing Joe off on Frank's motorcycle, Chet was called by Aunt Gertrude to the kitchen. She handed him a wrapped, warm box.

"What's this?" he asked.

"Since you're going into town, you won't mind dropping this cake off at Mrs. Bartlett's house on Kent Street, will you?"

"I'll be glad to."

When Chet reached the business district, he pulled his jalopy over to the curb. "Guess I'll deliver the cake later," he said to himself. Chet felt very empty. "Should've had a bigger lunch."

He squared his shoulders and took out a list of Bayport markets supplied by local farmers. He hoped to pick up the trail of the Birnham's produce truck.

"Guess I'll start with Max's Supermarket." From his pocket he took out some watercress and munched on it.

There was no red truck bearing the name Birnham at the large, block-long store. Chet drove on to the Food Fresh Market three blocks away. Seeing only a blue truck unloading vegetables, he headed farther down the street to a smaller store. He checked vehicles parked at the rear. No luck.

Back in his jalopy, Chet looked longingly at a pork-roll sandwich stand crowded with customers.

"Boy! I could go for a nice, juicy, well-done . . . " Quickly he drove out of sight of the stand.

At Castagna's Grocery near the waterfront, Chet

obtained the names of stores usually supplied by the Dodds' now jobless truck driver.

"These must be some of the places giving Birnham business now," the youth concluded, stuffing the list into his pocket. In the car again, he spread the paper out on the front seat, moving Aunt Gertrude's cakebox over. For a moment he eyed it hungrily, then drove off.

By two-thirty he had covered five of the nine listed stores without seeing the red truck. He shut off the motor and relaxed. His stomach rumbled. "Should have eaten something at the Hardys'," he thought, and again looked at the cakebox.

Taking out a pencil, Chet crossed out the stores and markets he had already covered. He sighed wearily.

"The vegetable deliveries may be over for today. Wonder what kind of cake Aunt Gertrude made. Four places to go. Wonder . . ."

He lifted the lid of the white box and sniffed. "Chocolate fudge—my favorite!" He sighed, then started the motor and proceeded to Frankel's Market.

"Birnham's truck just left here," the manager told him. "About five to ten minutes ago. I think he goes to a place on the west side of town after us."

"That must be the other Food Fresh store," Chet thought. Getting into the hot car, he again sniffed the cakebox. Slipping the string off, he opened the cover, and beheld the luscious whipped chocolate frosting. His stomach growled as he wiped his forehead. "Maybe a little taste—"

Finding a large gob of frosting that had fallen off he thumbed it. Carefully he picked it up and laid it on his tongue. "*Mmm*," he murmured.

When Chet reached the Food Fresh Market on Kennedy Street, he learned that the Birnham truck had not yet made its delivery. The man in charge of the produce department told him it was uncertain when the truck would come.

"Guess I'll wait," Chet said, but almost immediately returned to the car. Untying the string again, he took a small dab of frosting.

After half and hour Chet got out, stretched, and paced back and forth in front of a restaurant. Then he got back in. He felt weak with hunger.

The car was very warm. As the cake frosting became stickier in the heat, occasional breezes wafted its fragrance to Chet's nostrils. He opened the box. "Just one more lick."

By now, he had eaten all the uneven gobs of chocolate. Chet sighed. Slowly he ran his finger lightly around the cake in a complete revolution, chuckling. "Mrs. Bartlett won't even notice."

After licking the frosting off his thumb, he studied the cake again. One part of the swath he had made was wider then the rest. With his finger he made another circuit to even the groove, but

in his eagerness dug in too deeply at one place.
"Uh-oh, now I've done it!" he moaned.

Glancing out the window, he still saw no sign
of the red truck. His eyes returned to the inviting
cake. "Can't just leave it that way, he mused. Then
he swallowed. "Morton, get hold of yourself!"

Chet got out and plodded to and fro. No red
truck. Sighing, he climbed into the front seat and
uncovered the cakebox again.

"If I just cut off that little gouged piece, I can
tell Mrs. Bartlett I snitched a tiny bit."

Chet sat back, tucked a handkerchief into his
T-shirt, and having no knife, made a small wedge
of two pudgy fingers to push down through the
thick, melting frosting. A minute later his hands
and chin were daubed with chocolate. The hungry
boy surveyed the damage.

Several thumbprints surrounded the drooping
surface near the small missing segment. Besides,
his fingers had cut wider and wider on their paths
toward the plate.

"Got to even it off."

Twenty minutes later Chet was still evening
up the wedge and making it larger and larger.
Suddenly he heard a heavy motor and saw a huge,
red truck marked BIRNHAM pull into an alley
next to the store. He climbed out and crossed the
street.

Chet leaned heavily against a mailbox. He had
a clear view of the back end of the truck as it was

unloaded by the driver and two store employees. This appeared to be the truck's final delivery, for its eight or ten remaining vegetable crates were removed and taken into the store.

"That truck's big enough to carry two cars all right," he said to himself.

The tough-looking driver started the motor and began backing out. Chet hastened to his car, his stomach feeling a bit uncomfortable. Behind the wheel, he loosened his belt.

"Wonder where that driver's going," Chet thought.

A block from Barmet Bay he saw the produce van pull into a large, dilapidated, brown-shingle warehouse surrounded by a vast, junk-filled lot. The faded sign over the door read. KITCHER'S JUNKYARD.

Chet cut his ratchety engine and looked warily up the street toward the building. He heard the truck door slam.

"What could Birnham have to do with a run-down place like this?" he wondered.

Chet decided to take a closer look and shuffled up the street. Nobody was in sight at the wide entrance. Swallowing dryly, Chet hitched his trousers up, and after peeking in the warehouse, tiptoed inside.

The faint murmur of voices came to him from behind a closed door to the rear. Next to the parked truck was a black sedan Chet recognized as the one driven by Slagel. He peered in its rear window.

On the floor lay a small, vinyl phonograph record near a small generator. "A clue! I'll give it to Frank and Joe." After glancing toward the office, he reached in and picked up the disk, then slid it inside his T-shirt.

Chet turned to the musty flaps on the back of the truck. His face red with exertion, he clambered up and squeezed through the flap opening, letting some light into the rank-smelling interior.

On the stained, bare floor were scattered splinters of wood and random, rotted greens. "If these vegetables don't prove to be clues," he thought, "I can use them for samples of botanical deterioration."

As he scooped the various greens into his pockets, Chet noticed, on the scratched floor, muddied, ridgelike patterns.

"Tire-tread marks!" he gasped.

Then he heard the voice of an approaching man, calling back to the office. "No, the kids'll fall for the trap. Slagel's waitin' out at Saucer Rock to take care of them!"

"Good night! Joe! Joe's out there!" Chet realized, suddenly feeling sweat on his forehead. His heart thumped wildly. "I must get back!"

Just then the truck flap flew open and light flooded the interior. Glaring in at him, Chet saw the hard face of a stocky, red-haired man!

CHAPTER XIV

Sea Clues

SAUCER Rock, a broad, flat overhang above a deserted dirt road outside Bayport, was known to most people in the vicinity. Joe reached the spot ten minutes before his appointed meeting with the Dodds.

Parking the motorcycle, he approached the large, sunlit, limestone rock and sat down on a smaller one underneath it. Then, thinking of a possible trap, he got up and walked around.

The surrounding woods were quiet except for the twitter of a few orioles. Joe looked at his watch. It was 12:35.

As Joe neared the overhang, a glittering object nearby caught his eye. Stooping, he picked it up.

"Jack's high school ring!"

At that instant a sound like crackling fire reached Joe's ears. Tensing, he noticed a large

Joe raced for safety

moving shadow engulfing his! He spun around to face Saucer Rock.

A station wagon was toppling off directly toward him!

Darting back, Joe barely escaped the plunging car. Then came a shattering crash. Pieces of broken glass flew by him, as he looked up the slope. The sound of rushing feet along a nearby road stopped with the slam of a car door. The motor roared off into the distance.

The roof of the toppled car, its three remaining wheels still spinning, was completely crushed in. A shudder passed through Joe. "It's the Dodds' station wagon!"

Fortunately, the vehicle was empty. Joe inspected some curious deposits on the fender. "Salt-water corrosion! I must report this!"

He ran to his motorcycle. After telephoning Chief Collig from a farmhouse, he drove home.

Frank returned from his trip moments later. He was stunned by his brother's story. "The men must have timed it, knowing we wouldn't have a chance to study the handwriting on the note. I hope Collig's men can nab them."

"I'll bet it was Slagel's work and now he'll probably lie low and keep away from his 'job' at Birnham's."

"What about your trip?" Joe asked. "Any luck?"

"Some. I saw several good used cars. We might buy one."

Just then the Hardys heard a familiar chugging sound in the driveway, then the heavy plodding of two feet through the kitchen and into the living room.

"Chet, how did it go?" Joe welcomed their friend. "Say, you don't look very happy."

"Joe, you're home! You're safe!" Chet exclaimed.

He collapsed into the large green armchair. "Whew! Have I got an earful for you fellows!"

Fanning himself with a magazine, Chet told the Hardys of his adventure. They leaned forward when he mentioned the junkyard.

"And when I saw this guy glaring at me, I decided it was now or never. So I landed on him."

"*Landed* on him?"

Chet nodded, pride swelling his chest. "Just took a run, sailed off the end of the truck, and knocked him off balance. Then I dashed to the car. He didn't know who I was, so nobody chased me."

Joe laughed. "It's a good thing you've been keeping in training on that diet."

"My—diet?" Chet gulped. "Oh yeah, that."

At Chet's report of the tire tracks inside the Birnham truck, Frank jumped up. "That proves it! The gang is shipping the hot cars into Bayport in that truck at night. Were there autos in the junk lot, Chet?"

"I never noticed. I did get these." Standing up,

Chet unloaded frayed, discolored greens on the coffee table. Frank was about to groan when Chet's eyes riveted on one of the greens. "Hey, this isn't produce—it's a piece of seaweed!"

"Seaweed?"

Chet checked his pocket-sized algology book. He nodded. "Yes. Not exactly seaweed, but it's a form of marine vegetation."

Joe recalled the salt-water traces he had detected on the crushed Dodd station wagon. When he related his findings to Frank and Chet, the three boys tried to correlate the two sea clues.

"I wonder—" Joe thought. But when he compared the sea leaf with the Pilgrim drawing, they proved to be dissimilar.

"The stolen car hideout—and maybe the place the Dodds are being held—must be somewhere not far from the ocean!" said Frank. "But where?"

"Probably north along the coast," Joe suggested. "There are miles of beach, but we've scouted most of it. The police have checked all the buildings, public and private, north of the Barmet beach area."

"How about the waterfront?" Frank asked.

"It's possible. But where could they hide cars, even repainted, right in the face of Collig's heavy police lookout?"

Again recalling the shipment mentioned in Slagel's telegram to Melliman, the Hardys decided to watch Kitcher's Junkyard that night.

Suddenly Chet remembered the small phonograph record. "Got something else," he told the others excitedly. He stood up and slipped it out of his T-shirt.

He groaned. The edges of the black vinyl disk had curled up from heat.

"I hope it will still play," Frank said, going to the record player.

From the speaker came the warped sound of a loud automobile collision!

"The collisions in the woods!" Joe exclaimed. "This must be how Slagel or his pals decoyed the police off the track—by playing this record and making them look for an accident instead of chasing a stolen car."

"The paint flecks must be part of the same idea!" added Frank.

The brothers poured thanks on Chet for his reconnaissance work. But his pride was being snuffed by the beginnings of a stomach-ache. As he rose to leave, he heard Aunt Gertrude's footsteps coming down the stairs.

"Well, guess I'll be leaving," he said quickly, almost sprinting to the back door.

But a friendly voice stopped him. "Oh, Chester"— Miss Hardy smiled—"I want to thank you for delivering my little gift to Mrs. Bartlett."

"Oh, I— Yes, I delivered it. I—I—"

"It was an errand I shouldn't have burdened you with, but she's a lovely woman, as you could see, and I always try to send her one of my chocolate-fudge cakes.

"Before you go," she continued, holding a second cake up to Chet's nose, "I *insist* you have a piece of Laura's delicious caramel cake. This silly diet of yours has gone far enough, and I know you like pecans and marshmallow fill—"

"Yes, yes," the youth muttered, and to the others' surprise rushed from the house.

That night Frank and Joe drove to the waterfront area, parking in a cobblestone alley behind a fish store. Their position afforded a good view of Kitcher's Junkyard.

"If there's any kind of a shipment here tonight, we should be able to spot it," Joe whispered from behind the wheel.

The air was cold. Damp gusts from the foggy bay, just visible down a small hill, chilled the air. Both boys shivered, having neglected to bring sweaters.

Through the mist a light was visible inside the junk warehouse. Occasionally a gaunt figure appeared in the light and lounged in the doorway.

"That's probably Kitcher," Frank said. A moment later it began to drizzle lightly.

A black sedan moved slowly down the street and parked in front of the junkyard. The brothers leaned forward as they recognized Slagel emerging from the car, its motor still running.

"Guess he's not staying long," Frank whispered.

Kitcher and several other men appeared in the light of the doorway and conversed with Slagel. The burly ex-convict shrugged. He held up his hand to the rain which by now was heavy, and shook his head. Then he returned to his car and drove off.

"Looks as if he doesn't plan to come back," Frank said. "Think we should follow?"

"I'd rather find out what's going on here," Joe answered. "I'd say Slagel's appearance proves that if there is to be a shipment, it will be to Kitcher's."

The street became silent, but the lights in the warehouse remained on. During the next hour Kitcher emerged several times to look at the rain. Another hour passed, then two. Except for the periodic drone of a distant foghorn, the only sound was that of gurgling gutters.

Shivering, the boys rolled up the windows, leaving them open a crack. Joe turned on the heater, hoping the engine noise would not give away their presence. After the car warmed up, they listened to the mesmerizing patter of raindrops on the roof. Soon Joe fell asleep.

Yawning, Frank kept his eyes fixed on the junkyard area, feeling more and more sleepy. He felt a sensation of dizziness when he nudged his brother to take the next shift.

"Come on—I'm falling off. Wake me in—Joe?"

His brother's eyes remained closed. Frank shook him more vigorously. "Joe!"

Feeling his own eyes dimming, Frank tried to rouse Joe. He could not awaken him. Panic seized him. Joe was unconscious and Frank felt himself slumping to the floor!

CHAPTER XV

Double Attack

DESPERATELY shaking his head, Frank pushed open the door and pulled his brother outside into the rain. Leaning against a wall, he breathed in large draughts of air.

Mumbling, Joe revived. "What happened?"

"Don't know, but I have a fair idea." Frank shut off the car motor and opened all the windows wide. "My guess is carbon monoxide."

"I don't get it. We left the windows open enough so we shouldn't have had that much CO inside."

"Somebody may have clogged our exhaust." Frank investigated but nothing was stuffed into it now.

The warehouse was dark. "I wonder when the men left," Joe said, disappointed.

The brothers crossed the silent, dark street. The warehouse door was locked, so the Hardys peered over the fence into the lot. The yard was strewn with junk, including numerous heaps of rusted piping and battered automobiles.

"Well, chalk off one wasted night," Joe said as they returned to the car.

"It wasn't exactly dull." Frank smiled. "I have a hunch our friends' shipment may come off tomorrow night. Maybe the weather changed Slagel's mind."

By late the next morning the weather had cleared. After wiring their father, the boys repaired the car exhaust which, they found, had been punctured in several places.

"I wonder when those crooks did this," said Frank. "Probably before we left here last night."

After lunch Frank and Joe drove out to the Dodd farm for their appointment with Martin Dodd. Parking near the barn, they got out and waited.

Presently Frank looked at his watch. "The professor should have been here by now."

Fifteen minutes later the brothers walked to the back of the house. Here the ground was still muddy from the previous night's rain. Frank pointed out a confused jumble of footprints and suddenly Joe stumbled on a hard object in the mud. Looking down, he gasped in alarm.

It was the broken half of a smashed telescope!

"The professor must have been in a scuffle!" he said. Nearby Frank found a dead bat. Both boys recalled the one they had seen on the beach some days before. "I may be crazy," said Joe, "but I wonder if somebody's leaving these dead bats around on purpose."

Finding no clues to Martin Dodd's whereabouts, Frank and Joe drove away. "I'm worried, Joe," said Frank. "If Slagel and his gang have captured the professor, every move we make may endanger the lives of three people."

"I wonder," Joe replied, "if the professor came upon a clue to the car hideout."

"Or the answer to the Pilgrim mystery," Frank added.

The Hardys stopped at headquarters to report the professor's seeming disappearance. Chief Collig was concerned, and said he would order his men to conduct a search. Back at the house, Frank and Joe found a coded telegram had arrived for them. "It's from Dad!" Joe said.

> BOYS—HAVE LEARNED WE ARE WORK-
> ING ON THE SAME CASE. MELLIMAN MEM-
> BER OF GANG SMUGGLING GAS, WEAPONS TO
> HIDDEN ARSENAL SOMEWHERE NEAR BAY-
> PORT. WATCH DOCKS.

"The same case!" Joe exclaimed. "Melliman's traffic in gases could explain the liquid gas."

Frank went for Slagel's telegram to Melliman and read the opening aloud:

"*More nerve now, trying for 8-cylinder stock.*"

The words seemed to take on a different meaning and a far graver one.

"Eight cylinders of nerve gas," Frank said grimly, "probably smuggled and then shipped up the coast to Slagel's gang!"

"That must be why Dad wants us to watch the docks!"

The young sleuths decided to watch both the junkyard and the docks that night. They phoned Chet and asked him to come over. When their stout friend arrived, he entered the crime lab hesitantly.

"You fellows been cooking up something?"

Joe grinned. "Chet, have you ever heard of the wooden horse?"

"Sure. Wasn't that the roadblock the people of Troy used to keep out the attacking Greeks?"

"Not exactly." Frank laughed. "It was a huge gift from the Greeks to the Trojans. But they had really packed the horse with soldiers. When the Trojans accepted the gift, the Greeks were able to get inside the city walls and defeat them."

"What of it?" Chet shrugged.

"We have a similar plan." Frank clarified his remark. "We've decided that if everything else fails, there's one way we might blow this case wide open. That's to buy a car and allow it to be stolen!"

"Buy a car!" Chet exclaimed.

"Yes. Joe and I have enough money to buy a

secondhand sedan at Harpertown, where we're unknown. If it's flashy enough, Slagel's gang may steal it out on Shore Road—and us too. Our car will have a large trunk and we'll be in it!"

Chet shook his head. "And I suppose you'll ask me to drive it."

The Hardys grinned but did not answer. Instead, they said they wanted Chet to help them that evening. They would use Mr. Hardy's car.

By nine o'clock the car was parked between two automobiles a block away from the junkyard.

Presently Slagel arrived and great activity became evident around the lighted lot. Kitcher moved about, making notes on a clipboard as men carried metal junk inside the building. Melliman was nowhere in sight.

"I guess he works behind the scenes and is the brains of this whole operation," Frank whispered.

Soon several tow trucks bearing Kitcher's name rolled out of the warehouse and headed downhill toward the docks. Tied behind each of them were five battered cars.

"They couldn't be stolen," Chet said. "Nobody would buy them."

As the warehouse doors closed, the boys decided to follow the shipment and Frank drove off.

Reaching the docks, he parked near a row of steel drums, behind which the boys stationed themselves.

The lights of a barge glittered in the waters of

Barmet Bay. The name *Arachne* was painted on its side in white letters. The dilapidated cars were being unhitched from the tow trucks and rolled toward the barge.

In an hour all the junk cars had been loaded onto the barge. Several loads of rusted wire and sheet metal followed. Slagel and Kitcher returned to their car. A whistle sounded over the churning water, then slowly the *Arachne* backed into the dark bay toward the south.

"Come on. Let's take the *Sleuth!*" Frank motioned.

The boys reached the Hardy boathouse in record time. A minute later the *Sleuth's* motor roared to life. A night wind fluttered at their backs as they reached the mouth of Barmet Bay. Joe peered through field glasses.

"There it is!" he cried out.

The lights of the *Arachne* moved slowly down the coast. Her bow and stern lamps off, the *Sleuth* increased speed. When Frank had swung farther out to sea he headed parallel to the coast. Abreast of the barge, he throttled down to six knots.

"We can't do this forever!" Chet protested. "They'll catch on!"

Frank slipped off his shoes. "I'm getting a closer look at what and who's on that barge."

"You're crazy!" Joe protested. "You wouldn't have a chance against all of them!"

"I'll be careful. Keep the *Sleuth* on course and give me about twenty minutes."

Before Joe could say more, Frank was overboard and swimming toward the ghostly lights. He was midway between the two crafts when Joe saw the black fishing boat. Joe stiffened with fear as he deciphered the international code message which was being flashed by lights from the fishing boat to the barge.

"*O-n-e o-f H-a-r-d-y k-i-d-s s-w-i-m-m-i-n-g t-o-w-a-r-d y-o-u. S-t-o-p h-i-m.*"

Joe jumped into the water instantly and swam toward his brother. Frank, fighting strong currents, had not noticed the warning. Minutes later, he reached the barge and caught his breath. Then, grasping the damp wood with his wet hands, he pulled himself up and slid noiselessly over the side next to a braced car.

Suddenly someone struck him a hard blow on the head. His next sensation was of falling to the water. Frank blacked out before he reached it, but revived as he felt two arms grab him and take him to the surface.

Desperately, Joe bore his brother through the waves to the darkened *Sleuth* as the noise of the barge motors became fainter and fainter.

Joe was almost at the end of his strength when he touched the hull of the *Sleuth*. Chet leaned over and hauled Frank, semiconscious, aboard.

The next instant, Joe heard Chet cry out and saw him topple backward out of sight.

Grabbing the rail, Joe swung into the stern of the boat. To his horror, Chet lay motionless beside Frank. Joe whirled to face the attacker—a muscular, black figure in a glistening skin-diving suit.

The man raised a sharp, dripping piton and lunged at Joe!

CHAPTER XVI

Retreat Trick

BLOCKING the thrust of the spike, Joe threw all his remaining strength into a hard-fisted uppercut. The blow sent the diver reeling against the fantail of the *Sleuth*. Staggering, the black figure noticed Chet beginning to revive. In a flash he dived overboard and disappeared.

Joe hurried over to Frank, who by now was sitting up groggily. "Thank goodness you're all right," he said. "Chet, you okay?"

Chet winced and rubbed his jaw, but smiled gamely. "You Hardys are the ones I'm worried about!"

"You can't keep us down!" Joe said with a grin as he helped Frank to his feet.

"Thanks for saving my wet skin," Frank said.

Shivering, Joe crouched out of the wind and started the engine. He pointed to starboard. "Look!"

Fifty yards away the fishing boat idled in the

waves, its lights extinguished. Through the darkness, the boy could see its pilot pulling another figure aboard. Then the boat sped in the direction of Bayport.

"Let's go!" Frank said.

The *Sleuth* followed. It was just closing the gap near the mouth of Barmet Bay when the motor began sputtering. The gas gauge read empty. In disgust the boys watched the black boat vanish down the coast.

"How are we going to make the boathouse?" Chet asked nervously.

Frank pointed to the emergency oars. "The tide's coming in, so that'll help us row."

Joe was angry about the fishing boat and its occupants getting away. Frank consoled him. "At least we've learned the owner of that boat is in on this racket. Also, I'm sure we had our first meeting with the spider-man!"

"Who?" chorused Joe and Chet.

"The skin diver—he's powerful enough to scale cliffs. And that pike he had is used for mountain climbing."

Chet shuddered. "Or a weapon."

"He's the one who trapped Callie in the net," Joe added.

Frank expressed disappointment at his failure to get a look aboard the barge or at the man who had knocked him into the water. "We'll have to tackle the problem from another angle."

"Not tonight!" Chet begged. "We've had enough."

The Hardys agreed and the boys rowed wearily to the boathouse.

First thing the next morning Frank checked with police headquarters. There were no leads to any of the missing Dodds. The brothers were discussing what move they should make next, when the telephone rang. It was Tony Prito. He excitedly asked the boys to come to the *Napoli's* boathouse at once. "It's important!"

When they met him, Joe asked, "What's up?"

"Can't tell you yet." Their friend, wearing swimming trunks, hurried them aboard his motorboat and steered north out of Barmet Bay. He slowed down just past Bay Bluff.

"I think I saw something out here yesterday, and if it's what I suspect—"

Tony headed toward the shoreline, studying the water closely. Suddenly he cut the motor and leaned over the side. The Hardys followed his pointing finger.

"Down there!"

Beneath the gray surface of the water, a slight glimmer of light was visible. Straining their eyes, Frank and Joe could make out part of a green-and-white object. Their hearts jumped.

"Jack's boat!" Frank exclaimed. "Do you think—" He did not voice the dreadful thought that crossed each boy's mind.

Tony said tersely. "We won't know until one of us goes down there. I'll go!"

Tensely Frank and Joe watched Tony's lithe body cut the water and his distorted image vanish into the depths. They waited in grim silence.

When Tony's head broke the surface, the look on his face brought vast relief to the Hardys. "It's the Dodds' boat all right, but nobody's in it." He climbed aboard the *Napoli*. "Do you think their kidnappers scuttled it?"

"Probably," Frank guessed, "they wanted the boat out of the way so that the police would think the Dodds had escaped in it. We'd better report this right away."

Tony drove back to Bayport and the brothers went home. They had just entered the kitchen door when the telephone rang. Joe answered it.

"Joe Hardy speaking."

The voice at the other end said crisply:

"Kid, you and your brother have meddled enough. If you ever want to see your friends alive again, get out of town and stay out for five days—it might be good for your mother's and aunt's health too. This is your last warning! And be sure to take a look out your front window before leaving."

When Joe heard the receiver click, he hung up and told Frank of the threat. "It was Slagel, I'm sure."

The brothers ran to the front windows.

Between two trees along their quiet street, a black sedan was parked. Two strangers sat silently in the front seat watching the Hardy house.

Joe was upset. "We can't just obey Slagel—but we can't ignore a threat to Mother and Aunt Gertrude, either. What choice have we? Maybe we should call the police."

Frank thought a minute, then his eyes lighted up. "Not yet, Joe. Let's try our wooden-horse operation!"

The boys suddenly realized how well their secret plan would work during the present predicament. Joe led the way upstairs. "Of course! If we leave now for Harpertown, we could buy the car while we're 'vacationing.' And then—" he grinned—"gallop into Troy!"

The boys brought down suitcases from the attic and packed them hastily. While Frank changed into Bermuda shorts and a light jacket, Joe opened a closet and brought out a fishing rod, surfboard, and an air mattress. "We may as well make it look good."

Frank was sober. "We'll have to let Mother and Aunt Gertrude know why we're leaving, but I hate to worry them."

"We'll have to tell them for their own safety. Besides, it's the best reason we've had for a vacation in a long while!"

Twenty minutes later, their bags and gear at the foot of the stairs, the brothers went into the kitchen and told the two women of the threat. "But we'll be able to return to Bayport in less a week," Joe added.

"We'll phone you as often as we can," Frank assured them. "It will be the only way for us to know you're both safe."

Mrs. Hardy's pretty face showed worry, but she forced a smile and kissed them. "Frank—Joe— take care of yourselves. You promise you'll be able to return in a few days?"

"We may be home sooner than you think." Joe chuckled.

Aunt Gertrude's face wore an expression of militance. Removing her apron, she took a large frying pan off a hook.

"Just where are these two men watching our house?" she asked, brandishing her weapon. "Who do they think they are, threatening my nephews!"

It took Laura Hardy's help to restrain their courageous relative from marching outside. Finally she replaced the frying pan.

"Aunty," said Frank, "this isn't really a Hardy retreat. It's sort of a strategic withdrawal."

The boys made two quick telephone calls, one to Chet, and the other to telegraph their father. Then they took some cash which they kept in the house safe. Picking up a suitcase, Frank turned to Miss Hardy. "Aunty, you and Mother can help by showing a lot of emotion out at the car. We want to impress those men."

The two women did their part. When the boys had loaded all their luggage and vacation equipment into their father's car, Mrs. Hardy embraced them fervently. Aunt Gertrude's eyes were red as from weeping. In each hand she held a concealed onion. From their car, the two men watched the well-staged scene.

Amidst much waving Frank and Joe pulled down the driveway and drove up the street. The black sedan moved out and followed.

When the boys reached the highway beyond the city limits, Joe glanced back at the car following. "Next stop Harpertown," he said. "Then the wooden horse!"

CHAPTER XVII

The Wooden Horse

FRANK kept the car at a leisurely speed. In the rearview mirror he and Joe could see the black sedan fifty yards behind them.

"If we go any faster," said Frank, "those men will think we're trying to shake them. I want them to keep thinking we're just going on a vacation."

Using Route 10 and then the State Highway, the Hardys rolled along toward their destination. They had ten miles to go when Joe murmured, "They're still trailing us."

In Harpertown the Hardys headed for the beach resort area. Soon they drew up before a large seaside motel.

Frank took several bills out of his wallet and handed them to Joe. "We'd better pay for a week to make it look good."

Frank stayed behind the wheel while Joe went

in to register. When he came out again, they took their luggage from the trunk.

"Our friends are still along," Frank whispered.

Joe could see the black sedan parked to their rear half a block away. Paying no attention, the boys carried their gear in two trips up to their second-floor room. On the last trip, Joe overheard the sedan's driver checking the Hardys' length of stay with the desk clerk.

In the room the boys changed into swimming trunks. "It's a shame we can't enjoy what we paid for." Frank smiled. "But we'll put on a good act for our two friends."

When the Hardys returned from a brief swim, the black car was gone. "Think we've convinced them?" Joe asked.

"Yes. They're probably hightailing it back to Bayport to attend to their—er—business."

It was early afternoon when the brothers walked to a used-car lot in the Harpertown business district—the one Frank had scouted on his previous visit.

They looked over several late-model cars. Joe smiled. "It doesn't seem possible we're actually going to own a car."

"You're right."

The heavy, round-faced owner approached them. His manner was friendly and he talked volubly.

"Thought I remembered one of you fellows,"

he said, walking around with them. "What kind of car are you looking for?"

"Something pretty flashy, if it's not too expensive," Frank said.

"At least a year old," Joe added, recalling the points common to the cars stolen on Shore Road. "And nothing foreign."

The man knit his brows, then pointed out several large cars. He came to the end of a row. "Here's a nice Booster six-cylinder job, white walls, power steering—"

The boys regarded the two-tone brown sedan, then shook their heads. "None of these are as sharp-looking as we wanted. Have you anything else?"

The owner led them to a far corner of the lot. He pointed to a handsome, sea-green Chancellor, a model two years old. Excited, both boys walked around it several times.

"She's a real limousine all right," the dealer acknowledged. "But her engine's not the best and the carburetor could use some work. Wouldn't buy her myself, but if you boys want a flashy car, that's the one."

The Hardys climbed inside, then got out again. There was no question of the car's luxurious appearance.

Excited, Joe looked at his brother. "What do you think?"

Frank checked the trunk before replying, then

grinned. "I think we've found our horse!" Frank exclaimed. He turned to the man. "What are you asking for her?"

"I'll give you a fair price."

An hour later the Hardys happily closed the deal on the Chancellor. They had the bill of sale and new license plates. As the boys proudly received the keys and got in, with Frank at the wheel, the man leaned in the window.

"Can't understand why you care just about the car's appearance. But I wish you lots of luck." He started away, then looked back. "By the way, if you fellows are heading south, you'd better watch this baby near the Bridgewater-Bayport area. Been lots of thefts down there, and this is the sort of car they've been taking."

"Thanks for the tip."

Back at the motel, Frank and Joe rechecked the entire parking area for the black sedan. But it seemed to be gone for good. They now locked their father's car securely. "We'll have to leave this here in case those men return," Frank said. In their own handsome car, they were soon on the road back to Bayport.

"How does she drive?" Joe asked.

"A little slow starting. Otherwise, no trouble. After paying for a 'week's vacation' and a risky purchase, do you know how much money we have left?" Frank shook his pocket. "Three dollars and forty-seven cents!"

"Not much for a sleuthing trip," Joe commented. He traded places to try the car.

Frank switched on the radio in time to hear the end of a news bulletin.

"The car had been parked near a public-telephone booth at Ocean Bluff on Shore Road."

"Slagel's men are still in operation. That's a good sign—for us, anyway," Frank remarked.

The Hardys stopped along the highway at a small diner for a quick bite to eat, then phoned Chet. He promised to meet them in his car near a Shore Road camping area.

Dusk was falling when his jalopy rattled to a stop near their car behind some trees at the Pinewood Campsite.

"Jumpin' catfish!" he exclaimed. "She's a real beauty!"

The Hardys gave him the details of their being followed and the purchase. They directed Chet to park his car in an inconspicuous spot on the other side of the highway.

The boys' plan, though dangerous, was simple. If one of the gang took the "bait" and drove off in the Hardys' new car unaware of the brothers in the trunk, Chet was to follow cautiously at some distance. When he was sure of the thief's destination, he was to notify the police as quickly as possible.

"Of course I know the *real* reason you guys want my car parked over here." Chet winked as the

Hardys wished him good luck at his post. "You're afraid my four-wheeler will tempt Slagel's man away from yours."

Joe grinned. "Fat chance."

When darkness fell, the brothers climbed inside the trunk of their car and closed it. Joe had punched minute air holes in the metal near the seams. Although the air was very close, Frank and Joe were too tense to notice any discomfort.

Several hours passed, as they crouched in rigid silence. The only sounds were those of cars passing north and south on Shore Road.

The luminous dial on Frank's watch read one-thirty when they detected approaching footsteps. The Hardys stiffened.

The crunch of feet on gravel became louder, then stopped. After a silence, the boys felt the car door being opened and an added weight in front. Joe bit his lips.

The motor turned over weakly, sputtered, and died.

Several more attempts were made, but the engine only whined futilely. Both boys recognized the voice of Slagel complaining loudly. The car door slammed and the man's footsteps faded away.

The Hardys were bitterly disappointed. When they were sure Slagel had gone, the boys climbed out. "Guess that ends our wooden-horse bit tonight," said Joe in disgust as they signaled to Chet by flashlight to join them.

"What a bad break!" their friend said. "Can we try again tomorrow night?"

"You bet!" Frank answered. "Next time this car won't fail us! By the way, can we borrow a little money from you to tide us over?"

"Sure thing, but I only have ten dollars."

Tired and stiff, the Hardys primed the motor and reluctantly it started. They bid good night to Chet and drove back to their motel in Harpertown. In the morning they had breakfast and attended church. The Hardys spent the balance of the day working on the car engine.

Periodically they listened to radio newscasts, but there was no report of thefts.

After supper the brothers set out once more. "Cross your fingers and hope this car will be stolen!" Frank said as they left Harpertown.

The three boys had decided upon another spot for their mission—near a deserted fishing area on Shore Road somewhat south of the place used the previous evening. Chet arrived and took up his position in the dark woods.

This time Joe had placed an air mattress on the floor of the trunk and each carried a flashlight. As the Hardys climbed in, threatening storm clouds blotted the night sky. They snapped down the lid. Again the brothers imposed a rigid silence upon themselves.

Few cars came by, and only the faint sound of the sea reached their ears during the slowly passing

Would the boys' plan to capture the car thief work?

hours. Once Frank and Joe heard the voices of two night fishermen on their way down to the beach. Then it was still again. A boat whistle tooted mournfully from far out on the bay. Another hour dragged by.

A car approached, slowed down, and stopped. Then a door opened and shut quietly before heavy footsteps came toward the hidden boys. After a pause, Frank and Joe heard the front door of their own car close. They waited in an agony of suspense. Would the boys' plan to capture the thieves work?

The engine roared to life!

In a moment the boys' car was being backed up. Then it spun around and headed south on Shore Road. About a mile farther on, the Hardys braced themselves as the car turned sharply and headed in the opposite direction.

Frank held up his fingers in the shape of a V and grinned. The brothers tried to detect the sound of Chet's rattling jalopy to their rear, but could not do so above the noise of their own engine.

Joe watched the second hand of his watch, trying to estimate the distance north the car was covering. After eight minutes had passed, they slowed down. Frank heard a loud rattling sound like that of machinery. "A tractor!" he thought, and hastily whispered:

"Birnham's farm!"

It soon became clear that the car was not continuing toward Pembroke Road, Route 7, or Springer Road. Remembering Birnham's dirt lane, both Hardys anticipated entering this. But instead, the car slowed almost to a stop, then veered sharply to the left and began to bounce up and down, apparently going over bumpy terrain. At one point, Joe grimaced as his head struck the trunk lid. After a time the car hit a short, smooth stretch, then went downhill before the driver stopped and let the motor idle.

The Hardys heard a man say, "Okay in the gully!"

The boys were thrown forward as the car resumed its descent, and the roar of the ocean became louder. Their next sensation was of a soft, smooth surface before the car came to a halt. The engine was shut off.

"Nice work, Ben. She's a pretty one. Where'd you pick her up?"

"About five miles south—a real cinch."

"Anything valuable in the trunk?"

"Don't know. Didn't have time to check. Let's take a look."

A sinking feeling came over the Hardy boys! Holding their breaths, they clenched their flashlights.

The key was inserted into the lock of the trunk!

CHAPTER XVIII

Prisoner Rescue

FRANK and Joe crouched in the trunk, poised to defend themselves. At that moment there came a call from a distance, then the scrape of the key being withdrawn.

"We'd better go," said one of the men.

After their footsteps had faded, all was silent.

"Let's get out of here before they come back!" Frank whispered.

Raising the lid, the brothers climbed out and found themselves in darkness. They stood on the beach.

"This is where that black fishing boat docks!" Joe whispered. "It's anchored out in the cove now!"

As the boys watched it, Frank said, "We cased this inlet from the *Sleuth* and didn't see anything suspicious."

The brothers crouched behind upjutting rocks and beamed their lights upward. There was a short gully from the beach to the grassy slope.

"Look!" Frank hissed.

Pegged into the soil near the foot of the slope was the end of a long stretch of thick netting.

"It must go to the top!" he said. "That's how they get the stolen cars down! The net would give the cars traction. Slagel's Army hitch probably taught him this type of operation."

Frank reasoned that the bumpy part of the boys' trunk ride had been through Birnham's unplanted field to its far end. "To cover tire tracks of stolen cars pronto," he added, "the thieves had Birnham use his tractor and disk harrow over the ground. That explains his night farming. Next, the thieves crossed Shore Road for the descent and Birnham brushed away any tire tracks across the road."

Joe nodded. "The same truck must transport cars at night to Kitcher's before shipping them south of here—probably to New York. But that junk we saw put onto the barge puzzles me."

"Perhaps," Frank suggested, "Kitcher was moving it to make room for Slagel's booty."

"Let's find out where those men who brought us here went!" Joe urged.

Hugging the cliff base, the brothers proceeded in darkness along the beach. Presently they came to the mouth of a tunnel covered with hanging rockweed.

"No wonder we didn't know about this place," Joe whispered.

The boys noticed a strange odor of explosive powder and several dead bats.

"Dynamite!" said Frank. "It was probably what killed the bats we've found—one of them managed to fly as far as Oceanside Beach, the other died when it reached the Dodd farm. Slagel's gang must have enlarged this place to be used as headquarters."

A large rock just beyond the entrance apparently stood ready to be rolled into position as extra concealment for the mouth of the tunnel.

The boys, their eyes still on the launch, moved farther along the base of the sheer rock cliff hunting for additional evidence. Joe's eyes suddenly narrowed as he saw some mossy vegetation near a cluster of rocky projections. Wading out, he halted and covering the beam of his flash with his hands, held the light directly over the moss.

He was about to nudge Frank when they heard a motor start. Joe put out his light. The black fishing boat, a lighted lamp in the stern, began to move to the dock.

"Quick! Behind these rocks!" Frank urged his brother.

The boys crouched as the boat glided in. After the craft was moored, two men jumped from it and walked toward the tunnel entrance. One was the belligerent fisherman. The other, in a black skin-diving suit, they recognized as the man who had attacked them in the *Sleuth*. When the two disappeared through the rockweed, the Hardys followed them up the passageway.

A hundred feet in, cold air carried the smell of fresh paint, and presently they began passing newly painted cars. As the Hardys proceeded, with flashlights off, each boy had the same thoughts: Were they about to solve the mystery of the stolen cars? Was Chet safely on his way to the police? Would the next few minutes lead them to the three Dodds?

Suddenly Frank detected footsteps to their rear. He grabbed Joe's shoulder and they threw themselves flat against the wall, holding their breaths so as not to make a sound.

The steps came abreast of them.

Slagel!

Fortunately, his light beam kept to the center of the tunnel and he soon passed ahead. As Joe breathed out again, he said, "That was close!"

"Too close!" Frank murmured.

Walking forward even more cautiously, the Hardys rounded a bend and sidestepped a pile of broken shale. At several places the passageway was roof-beamed against cave-ins. Chipped-out hollows in the walls held automobile tools and rifles.

The tunnel came to an end in a large chamber, dimly lighted. Frank and Joe slipped into a narrow side passage, where Frank spotted a small, natural peephole in the wall. He peered into the room.

Against the opposite wall three men lounged on boxes near a row of cots. One of them stopped reading a newspaper aloud. Next to them stood several glistening machine guns, an oddly designed mortar, and numerous stacks of lighter shoulder weapons.

"They must be the foreign arms Melliman is trading with Slagel in return for the cars," Joe thought as he took a turn at the peephole.

Suddenly the high-pitched whine of a sanding machine caught the boys' ears and they saw a workman in a spotted white jacket start removing paint from a large, new sedan. Near him another man was spraying a car with green paint.

Their appearance evoked Frank's excitement. He thought, "That cinches it—those battered-looking cars on the barge *were* stolen! Instead of just repainting them to look new, Melliman has the color changed and then has the cars made to look *worthless* without really damaging them, so he can fool the local police. No doubt he spruces them up again when they reach New York!"

Two cars along a side wall caught Joe's attention. He recognized the model and year of one as being similar to Jerry Gilroy's stolen car! "But this one looks really beat up!" The car was severely corroded by fire and rust.

"Anyway," Joe decided, "this explains why

brand-new cars weren't stolen. It's easier to damage a used car. But why do all this disguising? Melliman must think it's worthwhile. There's something more to this whole deal than we've figured out yet. Maybe the cars will be sold in a distant foreign market."

Slagel stood in the center of the cavern conversing with the skin diver. When the sanding machine was turned off, the boys heard Slagel refer to him as Reb. They also detected garbled voices below them but had no view of the speakers.

Having seen everything close at hand, the young detectives turned to the more important concern of trying to find the Dodds. Silently they moved off down the narrower side tunnel. Holding their arms before them, Frank and Joe found the passage widened only slightly, then ended at a blank rock wall. Frank switched on his flashlight for a moment and almost cried out.

Bound and gagged only inches from his foot lay Professor Martin Dodd!

The man's face showed astonishment and relief as Frank put a finger to his lips, then dropped down to untie the professor. At the same time, Frank felt a nudge from Joe who pointed. Against a side wall lay Jack Dodd and his father!

The boys rushed over to unbind them and remove the gags. Both looked thin and haggard from their ordeal, but their faces lit up as the Hardys helped them stand.

"But how—" Jack whispered.

Joe cut him off and murmured in his ear, "Chet should be on his way here with the police by now. Let's get outside before the fireworks begin. Is there another exit besides the main tunnel?"

"I'm afraid not."

"We'll have to chance it then," Joe said.

Mr. Dodd stumbled with his first step, his limbs weak from the tight ropes. He muffled a cough as he took a few steps to regain his strength. Then he nodded that he would be all right.

The Hardys switched off their flashlights. Martin Dodd and Frank led the way out, followed by Jack and his father. Joe took the rear.

They were halfway down the side passage when the glare of four flashlights almost blinded them. An affected voice rang out.

"Why, my friends the Hardy boys! And here I had thought you weren't interested in taking my confidential case!"

Melliman!

CHAPTER XIX

Hopeless Escape

CONFRONTED by a submachine-gun barrel, the Hardys and the Dodds were strong-armed by a dozen henchmen behind Melliman and shoved into the main cavern. The prisoners' hands were quickly tied while two thugs trained guns on them.

"A pity," Melliman began, "that you should work such a splendid plan—and have it all come to nothing! Your unexpected visit, I am afraid, causes us a certain inconvenience." His eyes glittered.

Slagel thrust himself in front of Frank and Joe and flashed the blade out of his cane. "You little punks! You've caused us more trouble than all the cops in the area! For two cents I'd—"

"No violence, Slagel!" snapped Melliman, restraining the gangster. "At least, not for the present."

He turned to several of the men, including the

159

husky skin diver the boys knew as the spider-man, and the red-haired man Chet had seen at Kitcher's. "Get the cars ready for barge transport south— we're moving everything out tonight. Reb, you and Montrose take the boat to Kitcher's dock. Wait for the barge, then send her here immediately to the inlet."

The diver nodded and ran down the tunnel to notify the fisherman.

Slagel voiced discontent. "Are we gonna close up shop just because a couple of kids—"

"We have no choice," Melliman cut in as four men hastily lined up the refinished cars for movement down the tunnel. "Unfortunately, the Hardys may have relatives and friends who know they gave up the generous vacation we urged them to take."

Slagel protested that a storm was brewing at sea, but the unctuous Melliman soon convinced him by saying. "The arms and tanks of nerve gas are yours to do with as you like."

"You double-crosser!" Slagel yelled. "You're not leavin' me to take the rap!"

The two finally agreed that the lethal gas would go on the barge as usual, carefully packed in the trunks of the cars, and accompanied by Melliman. Slagel and the other henchmen would head south in Birnham's large truck, taking the weapons with them. They would meet Melliman's barge in New

York. A thug was dispatched to inform Birnham of the evacuation of the hideout.

While Slagel and Melliman stood with two guards near the prisoners, three men worked quickly on one of the unfinished cars near the paint rack, removing two door windows, sanding down the hood, and replacing its new tires with old ones. Both Frank and Joe noticed one man applying peculiar reddish and black compounds to the roof and sides.

Slagel pointed his cane at the five captives. "What about a halfway trip for 'em on the barge?"

Melliman removed his spectacles. "For the Dodds and the esteemed professor, perhaps. It might prove diverting for the police to find their bodies washed ashore. But we reserve a *special* treatment for the famous Hardy boys."

Melliman turned to the guard holding the automatic weapon. "Take them all into the gas alcove."

As the Dodds were pushed into line behind them, Frank whispered to Joe, "Try to keep Melliman talking until Chet and the police arrive— it's our only chance!"

The prisoners were led past a trunk of gas masks into a small corner previously not visible to them. Joe felt a shiver when he saw twenty metal cylinders against the damp wall. Most were black or orange, and a few, near their nozzles, had round meters. He could barely make out their chemical symbols and some foreign words.

Since Melliman planned to take the Dodds on the barge, only the Hardys' legs were bound. One of the men ran to the tunnel entrance to watch for the incoming barge.

Frank spoke to Melliman. "Maybe you won't mind telling us why you framed the Dodds."

"Not at all." The man smiled. "We noticed the boy Jack often snooping along the coast around here. We couldn't afford to have him find our setup."

"So you had your spider-man sabotage his boat off Oceanside Beach?" Joe asked.

"Yes. Unfortunately, it didn't prove successful. Since your friends live on Shore Road, we conveniently made them suspects and—shall we say? —arranged for them to jump bail."

Immediately the Hardys realized that the gang had not known of the Dodd Pilgrim mystery when they captured the farmer and his son. They were surprised, therefore, when Jack said:

"I never got a chance to tell you fellows my ideas about the treasure clue. I had looked inland and thought I'd search along the coast." He frowned. "Guess I was wrong."

Frank was about to suggest that Jack say no more, when Melliman interrupted. "Oh, yes, my friends and I first learned about this treasure when the Dodds came here as our guests. Jack was rather heated about our understanding of his coast prowling and let it slip out. But since then, both he and his father have been uncooperative in sharing their family secret with us."

Frank changed the subject and asked Melliman, "What led you to postpone your car shipment last Thursday at Kitcher's docks?"

"The weather," Slagel put in, surprised to learn the boys had been there.

"Yes," Melliman said. "I conceived our ingenious car disguises, although my partner here has helped considerably with his knowledge of camouflage. I figured if his rust and char coatings did not wash off in rain, weather would be of no concern to us. Nevertheless, we have tarpaulins on the barge, and tonight's impending storm should cause us no difficulties."

"And the fisherman was a lookout along the coast for parked cars—just as Slagel was on his trips up and down Shore Road?" Joe asked.

"Exactly. Since terrain or circumstances sometimes presented problems, we also made use of Montrose's colleague, Reb, with his swimming and climbing abilities.

"And that's where the lamp signals from the fishing boat figured?"

"Yes. During daylight Montrose signaled tips to Slagel by his anchoring at various places off shore. As for the lamps, they made the boat easily identifiable at night."

Melliman grinned mockingly. "You recall the signals before Paul Revere's ride? One light if an attack was coming by land, two if by sea? When Slagel saw two flashes, he knew Reb had spotted the police or you boys on the water and stopped bringing any stolen cars down the hillside! Our spider-man was a good go-between."

"That's right," said Slagel. "And *I* left the brown paint flecks and car tracks to fool the police. But *I* was a fool to lose my glove on the beach."

Melliman remarked, "Birnham has been most helpful. He disked out the stolen car tracks from his field and brushed them off the road when we brought the cars down the slope. He had the idea of his car being 'stolen' to throw suspicion elsewhere. Birnham had already told us of this tunnel and cave, which were ideal for a smuggling operation. We blasted it out for our needs. His truck to transport shipments to Kitcher's and his blockades were effective too."

Joe glared at Melliman. "And you're bringing guns and nerve gases into the United States for use by subversive gangs?"

Melliman scowled. "You're too smart. But it won't help you now. You boys should have accepted that assignment I offered you—it would have taken you safely out of town. Even your illustrious detective father can't do you any good now. We have eluded him."

The Hardys were told that Slagel had sent two men to put the brothers, and later Scratch, to sleep with gas. "You and the old geezer were in our way."

"You didn't get our dad's car," Joe needled.

"True," said Slagel, but added he had thrown the dud grenade into the Hardys' lab, and shot at the boys in the plane. He and Reb had pushed the Dodds' station wagon off Saucer Rock. He himself had tied up the two fishermen, and strung the wire netting into which Joe had crashed. The skin diver had damaged Jack's boat.

When footsteps sounded in the tunnel, Martin Dodd turned to the boys and whispered, "I guess it's all over for us—and solving the Pilgrim mystery—but I want to thank you for—"

Frank was about to tell the professor of their hopes invested in Chet when three figures entered the chamber. Frank and Joe paled.

Held prisoner between two men stood Chet!

"This is the kid I saw in the truck at Kitcher's," one said. "He took our record. We just caught him at the top of the slope. Lucky thing, or he'd have brought the police."

"Aha, a loyal friend of the Hardys!" Melliman pushed the petrified Chet against the wall and turned to his captors. "Isn't the barge here yet?"

"Just comin' now."

"Good! Get these three Dodds out to the beach.

Then clear that car out of the entrance. It hasn't been coated yet. Next start these other autos down the tunnel. Quick!"

The Dodds were seized and led into the main tunnel. Chet and the brothers remained with Slagel, Melliman, and a fat, armed henchman.

"Well"—Melliman rubbed his hands—"we'll have to part company now. I've decided to let you boys enjoy your last hours here together! Slagel, have one of your men wire the remaining dynamite at the tunnel entrance."

Slagel snickered as Melliman went on, "Boys, we'll even provide a little atmosphere." He winked at the fat henchman and pointed to the three cylinders. "When we call, you'll know what to do."

After Melliman and Slagel had left, Chet turned dismally to Frank and Joe.

"I'm sorry, fellows. I wasn't quick enough. I was heading for my car when those creeps nabbed me."

"We're not cooked yet," Frank consoled him in a whisper as he watched the squat man guarding them. "We must get out of here! Joe, did you notice that two of those worn metal cylinders against the wall are different from the others?"

Joe glanced to his right. His eyes widened. "They're just plain oxygen!"

"Right. Probably from the spider-climber's aqualung gear. Melliman must have left them here because they're empty," Frank whispered. "But maybe our guard doesn't know that!"

Not only were the oxygen cylinders of the same height and black color as the ones containing poisonous gas, but their labels were not visible to the guard.

"Hey, cut out that talking!" the gunman barked. "I've got to listen to know when to blow that gas and leave this joint—fast!"

Actually he seemed to be paying little attention to the tied-up boys. After a moment Frank checked with Chet, then nodded to Joe.

Shuffling quickly to an upright position, Joe swung his body wildly, pretending to get his ropes up on the sharp rock. Instead, he bumped purposely into one of the oxygen cylinders and forcefully toppled it over. The slender metal valve at the top smashed hollowly against the stone. The rolling cylinder clattered along the ground. By the time the startled man had spun around, all three boys were coughing violently.

"You fools!" he cried. His eyes filled with fear, he hesitated. Then, cupping his mouth, he raced out of the cavern and down the tunnel.

Immediately Frank crawled to the painting area of the cavern. He turned on the abandoned sander, wincing as the ropes smoked and finally broke between his hands. In seconds he had untied the other boys.

"Let's get to the Dodds!" Joe urged. The boys

had just taken a step forward when three men rushed in from the tunnel. Though all of them wore white cloths over their faces, Frank recognized two as the fleeing guard and the surly fisherman named Montrose. The third wore a barge pilot's uniform.

He cried out, "Gas? There's no gas here! These kids tricked you!" The men pulled down their masks and advanced. "Let's finish 'em off right here!"

The boys were trapped!

CHAPTER XX

Roundup and Treasure

MONTROSE whipped out a blackjack and advanced on the boys. The next instant he felt himself yanked around. An iron fist crashed into his jaw and dropped him unconscious to the floor.

The astonished boys saw that his attacker was the bargeman who had ripped off a mask, revealing the face of Fenton Hardy! Over his shoulders were several coils of rope.

Losing no time, Joe rushed the equally astonished guard. Blocking a wild swing, he drove a punch into the man's solar plexus. He doubled up and fell to his knees.

"Quick! Let's get these men tied!" Frank urged. He grabbed the rope from his father and with Chet's help bound both men securely. Mr. Hardy gagged them.

Chet exclaimed, "Mr. Hardy, you're a magician! How did you ever—"

"When I got my sons' telegram about the wooden-horse plan I was just finishing the last stage of my undercover work on Melliman s operations. I thought you might need help, so I stowed away on that barge when it docked at Kitcher's to deliver smuggled arms that were going to Slagel."

Frank briefed the detective on the excitement of the past few hours. "But Chet never got to the police!"

Mr. Hardy smiled. "I have good news. They should be on their way here right now! When that man in the fishing boat signaled an emergency call to the barge, I kayoed the barge pilot, then borrowed his uniform and came ashore. But first I alerted the police over my short-wave radio to grab Kitcher and watch where the fishing boat headed."

"And then you heard the 'gas' alarm from this guard when you docked?" Joe asked.

"Right. One of the thugs on the beach suspected it might have been an empty oxygen tank you boys had knocked over. But when they took the precaution of putting handkerchiefs over their faces, it gave me a chance to come along undetected by doing the same thing."

Leaving the thugs securely tied, Mr. Hardy led the boys toward the beach.

"It's my guess," said Frank, "they have the Dodds in one of those cars they're loading onto the barge."

"Then we'll have to stand them off until Collig's men arrive!" his father said.

He and the boys halted just inside the entrance and peered out through the curtain of rockweed.

The barge rocked gently at the tip of the dock, its lights out. A few cars were already aboard. The Hardys' own automobile stood nearby, while Birnham's truck was parked at the end of the gully. Guns and crates were being loaded into it quickly, as black storm clouds rolled ominously over the scene.

"Do you think the gang's lookouts may spot the police?" Frank murmured.

"Could be," his father whispered. "How many routes are there off this beach?"

"Just one—that gully over there," Chet answered. "It connects with the grassy slope to the top of the cliff."

A short time later the barge was fully loaded. A man began untying its mooring rope.

Mr. Hardy fastened his handkerchief over his face. "I'm going to draw some of them into the tunnel. Think you boys can cause them a little trouble out there on the beach?"

"I'll handle the gully," Joe whispered.

"Chet and I will watch the barge," Frank offered.

When the boys had backed against the rock wall near the tunnel, the detective ran toward the barge and gave a muffled shout.

"Hey, quick, some of you guys give me a hand with these kids in here!"

At once several footsteps pounded down the ramp onto the dock. Mr. Hardy dashed back into the tunnel. In a moment four men raced in after him. At once Frank, Joe, and Chet sprang into action.

Joe ran toward Birnham's truck, which was guarded by two men. After landing a stunning punch to one thief's jaw, he blocked the other with an upturned crate. Like lightning Joe leaped to the right-front tire and drove his pocketknife deep into the thick rubber until it collapsed. Yanking out the knife, Joe bounded into the gully.

Meanwhile, Frank and Chet were sprinting to the barge ramp. As Frank glanced back, he saw Chet trip, and the stocky figure of Birnham rushing to tackle him. Chet threw him off, however, and Frank rushed onto the ramp. Two men on the barge charged him.

Sidestepping the larger thug, Frank recognized the second man as Montrose. The boatman raised a tire iron, but got no further as Frank's head rammed into his midriff. With a groan, Montrose toppled backward onto the dock.

The next second Frank felt a sharp blow on his shoulder and the two strong arms of Slagel dragged him out to the beach. Slagel thrashed at Frank with his cane and the two rolled over and over in the wet sand. Suddenly the sound of wailing sirens put an end to the struggle. Slagel leaped up and bolted toward the tunnel. At the same time came a shout. "Cops!"

Dazed, Frank staggered to his feet in time to see four men climb into the brothers' car and race it into the gully!

Searchlights flashed on the beach and policemen swarmed down the grass slope. Just then a figure darted past Frank onto the barge. *Melliman!* Before Frank was halfway up the ramp, Melliman had kicked out the tire braces of one of the cars and rolled the car over the edge into the water.

For an instant Frank wondered why. Then he thought, "The Dodds must be inside!"

Melliman now leaped aboard the adjacent fishing boat. By this time Frank was in the water swimming in the direction of the sinking vehicle. When he reached it, Frank could see the three helpless Dodds within. The water was rising rapidly. Frank pulled on a door, but the pressure against it was too great!

"Hold on!" he yelled.

Fortunately, two policemen had followed Frank. Together, they pulled the door open, yanked the Dodds out, and bore them safely through the rising waves to the beach.

Chief Collig rushed up. "Are you all okay?"

"Fine, thanks, sir," Jack gasped as he was cut

loose. His father and uncle, having swallowed some water, coughed violently but soon were able to stand up.

"The crooks escaped in our car!" Frank exclaimed, starting toward the gully.

Collig stopped him. "Your brother pulled a fast one on them. He waited at the top of the cliff until they were halfway up the slope, then unfastened the netting. As it slid down, they couldn't move, and our men caught them. Your dad, after tunneling up half the gang, also took care of this fellow with the cane. He was still out cold when we handcuffed him!"

Just then Joe ran up, his face flushed with excitement and relief at the Dodds' rescue. When Mr. Hardy joined the group, the others learned that Melliman had not escaped in the fishing boat. "Apparently he couldn't get it started."

"And why not?" asked a familiar voice with a proud ring in it.

"Chet!"

Soaked to the skin, Chet added, "A knowledge of botany goes a long way—especially in learning to knot seaweed into a boat propeller!"

By now, Slagel, Melliman, and the rest of the prisoners had been led away to police cars on the cliff above. Only Collig and another officer remained on the beach with the Hardys and Dodds. The tide was rolling in now, and jagged streaks of lightning could be seen.

"How can we ever thank you Hardys and Chet enough!" Mr. Dodd said.

Collig added, "You boys will be receiving a handsome reward for your work."

Joe's eyes glistened. "I think there's another case we're going to solve tonight—the Pilgrim mystery." He sloshed through the surf which had almost covered the beach. Chet, Frank, and the Dodds joined Joe as he pointed to some leaves along the cliff. Puzzled, Mr. Hardy and Collig watched from the remaining strip of dry sand.

"I noticed this algae earlier tonight, and if I'm not wrong, it matches the leaf in the Pilgrim message," Joe declared.

"You're right!" Jack exclaimed. "But the message seems to indicate a place on land."

"Maybe we've been on the wrong track," said Frank. "Professor Dodd, can you remember the last words of the clue?"

The tall professor knew them by heart. " *'Crash of countless breaking black—'* "

" *'Billows'!* Not willows!" Joe finished. "Waves would break in a hurricane as well as trees."

"Joe!" the professor cried excitedly. "My calculations on the position of Venus—which is now obscured by clouds—had led me to this area of the coast a short time before I was seized by Slagel's men!"

Chet pulled a soaked book from his pocket. "That growth is *chondrus crispus*—Irish moss."

Frank exclaimed, "It was several hundred years ago when the Pilgrim family perished! Since that time, this coastline may have fallen several feet and water may now cover the location of their shelter."

"Then there may be a cave in the slope near where we're standing!" Jack cried out.

Another streak of lightning could be seen in the distance and the waves were rising over the moss-covered rock.

"Let's look before the storm gets here!" Joe urged.

With flashlights turned on the scene by the men, the four boys kicked off their shoes, stripped to their shorts, and dived in. Suddenly Frank came up and shouted, "I see something!"

Chet, Jack, and Joe swam over to him. Then all four vanished beneath a rough wave. Twenty seconds later they surfaced, holding a heavy object. Treading water, they maneuvered the object to the beach.

It was a steel-bound wooden chest!

Excitedly they set it down in the sand beyond the incoming tide, as the rest of the group rushed up. The metal had rusted almost to powder, and several holes gaped through the rotting wood. With Joe's help, Jack raised the wobbly lid, and everyone stared in wonderment.

Piles of green and blue jewels, strings of ruby beads, and rotted pouches of gold coins glistened with sea water amid brown weeds and Irish moss. Near one corner lay a large, algae-covered object.

"Look!" Martin Dodd exclaimed excitedly.

It was a bottle! He handed it to Jack's father, who carefully unstoppered it and removed a long roll of worn papers. The others gathered around as he read the first words aloud:

" 'The Record of a Perilouf Voyage in Fearch of the Horfefhoe-Fhaped Inlet, in the Year of Our Lord 1647, by Eliaf Dodd.' "

"We've found it!" Jack exclaimed.

As a streak of lightning creased the black skies, Frank glanced up at the cliffs. Suddenly he cried out, "There's the answer to the clue's last words!"

At the next flash the others looked up at the glistening rock. It had all the appearance of a *vein of gold!*

Drenched but happy, everyone walked toward the brothers' car. Each of the four boys bore a corner of the chest. Frank and Joe wondered if any case as exciting as the one just solved would ever come their way. They were soon to find out, when challenged by *The Secret of the Caves.*

Frank now smiled at the Dodds. "How about a lift?"

"Only if you'll promise to share Thanksgiving with us this fall," Jack answered. "We're going to have a feast that would make our ancestors proud! And you're going to join us too, Chet. We'll even have a special seaweed menu for you!"

"No roast turkey and sweet potatoes and—" Joe asked.

"Or chocolate cake with frosting," Frank added.

Chet groaned. "Stop it! Anything but seaweed!"

THE HARDY BOYS

COLLECT ALL EIGHT BOOKS WITH NEWLY ILLUSTRATED COVERS IN THE HARDY BOYS SERIES, FEATURING FRANK AND JOE'S CRIME-SOLVING ADVENTURES!

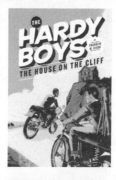

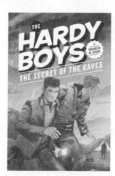

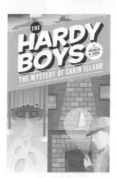